PSYCHOS
in love

S.J. RANSOM

WARNING...

THIS BOOK ENDS IN A CLIFFHANGER.

This book is the first in a series that will be following a reverse harem of characters. Please note that this book does end in a cliffhanger and that you will have to be patient all the way through to the end of the series to find out if there is a happy conclusion.

Now, if you are brave enough, turn the page and start the journey. You will encounter murder, kidnapping, rape, bondage, blood play, piss play, torture, angry violence, and descriptive scenes that may trigger you. You are going to find double penetration, choking, toy play, and BDSM themes. Everyone is over the age of eighteen. None of the characters are blood related. There is male on male action as well. This may not be your cup of tea and if it is not, I understand. But for those who wish to take this journey with me, enjoy...and welcome to the world of the Psychos.

WARNING...

THIS BOOK ENDS IN A CLIFFHANGER.

This book is the first in a series that will be following a reverse harem of characters. Please note that this book does end in a cliffhanger and that you will have to be patient all the way through to the end of the series to find out if there is a happy conclusion.

Now, if you are brave enough, turn the page and start the journey. You will encounter murder, kidnapping, rape, bondage, blood play, piss play, torture, angry violence, and descriptive scenes that may trigger you. You are going to find double penetration, choking, toy play, and BDSM themes. Everyone is over the age of eighteen. None of the characters are blood related. There is male on male action as well. This may not be your cup of tea and if it is not, I understand. But for those who wish to take this journey with me, enjoy...and welcome to the world of the Psychos.

This book is dedicated to my cousin, B. You know who you are. You were with me the entire journey cheering me on and telling me to keep writing. To make this a reality. And I did.

Thank you!

Psychos in Love Blurb

Charlotte

I shouldn't have witnessed the murders.
But I did.
And now I can't escape the men who want nothing more than to make me pay for being in the wrong place at the wrong time.
Kronos, Hypnos, and Ayres hold my life in their hands. And they just so happen to live by the motto of Leave No Witnesses.
They are psychos who love nothing more than death and destruction, but for some reason I've intrigued them enough to be kept as their pet.
They want my submission but I'll do anything to get my freedom.

Kronos

I'm under her spell as she struggles to break free.
Her eyes haunt me in ways I've never experienced.
But she's the sole witness to our crime and she has to die.
Eventually.
Right now all I can think about is sinking my cock inside of her, claiming her for all of eternity.
Am I crazy?
Fuck yes, I am.
Especially when it comes to her.

Hypnos

I instantly fell for her but no one needs to know that.
She's smart—too smart for her own good.
The moment she tried to fight us, my heart woke up from its dull existence.
There was no satiating my desire for her once I took her virginity with my tongue.

Ayres

I shouldn't have called her Kitten.
I most certainly shouldn't have wanted her to call me Daddy.
But those sorrowful eyes nagged at me in unexplainable ways.
My own demise from keeping my distance from her dissipated the moment she gave herself to me.
Unwillingly?
Yes, but she liked it.

Psychos in Love follows Charlotte and her capture and torture—and her internal struggle with enjoying almost every minute of it—at the hands of three men who want her dead...but not bad enough to kill their little pet.

PLAYLIST

Blood in the Water by Grandson
Watch Me Burn by Michele Morrone
Skin Deep by Memory of a Melody
Monster by Meg Myers
Overwhelmed by Royal & the Serpent
Middle Finger by Bohnes
Give'em Hell by Everybody Loves an Outlaw
Despicable by Grandson
Ashes by Stellar
Desire by Meg Meyers
Lost in Translation by Alice Kristiansen
Without the Light by Elliot Moss
Play with Fire by Sam Tinnesz, Yacht Money
Scream by Once Monsters
Sorry by Meg Meyers
I Don't Care About You by Missio
Serial Killer by Moncrieff, JUDGE
Horns by Bryce Fox
Do It for Me by Rosenfield
Cravin' by Stileto, Kendyle Paige
Scars by Boy Epic
Madness by Ruelle
Sociopath by Stayloose, Bryce Fox
Nightmares by Ellise

One

CHARLOTTE

Ten Years Earlier

"Mom, why are we leaving town?" I asked for the hundredth time. It didn't make sense to me that we would pick up and leave in the middle of the night. That was what we were doing, per my mother. My beautiful mother laughed at me as I fidgeted in the backseat, I continued to pester her with questions, and she sighed, shaking her head.

"Char, it's a surprise all right?" She turned to look at me and I could tell she needed sleep. I nodded. That exasperated tone told me I needed to learn to be patient. It was one of my downfalls. She smiled and bopped my nose like she always did when she wanted me to drop a topic we were discussing. I smiled back at her, taking her hand in mine.

"All right Momma," I whispered as the music in the car washed over us. We drove around a sharp, ninety-degree angle corner and a car came barreling straight toward us. Plowing us over, the sound of crunching metal turned my world upside down. My happy moment, obliterated. My world shifted from an innocent ride to incessant screams and shattering glass shards flying all around me.

"Momma?" There was no response. I screamed her name until my throat was sore. Why wasn't my mother answering me? What was happening? We kept flipping over and over. Motion sickness sat in, and I began to vomit as we landed upside down. I turned my head to the side to let the vomit flow down the window. All I could think about were piercing green eyes I saw in the other car.

I had never seen such eyes before. My mind wouldn't let the image go. The sadistic satisfaction from them chilled me to my bones. His face cemented itself into my memory. The reward of a photographic memory, I guess. I didn't know why I kept his gaze. *That's not true.* I knew exactly why I did it. He grounded me as the car kept doing cartwheels. That was crazy right?

The laughter and screams died down. *Had those come from me? From the other car? Was I dead?* So many questions filtered through my toggled brain. It was unfortunate that I didn't have the answers I needed.

"Hey ... Help ..." My screams went unanswered. My pleas laid against thin air. Two guys climbed out of the other car. My neck twisted in a weird angle, I couldn't see my mother. "M ... Momma?" Silence met me as I watched the guy from the back-seat of the other car throw a girl to the ground.

Vomit ran down my chin as I watched him break her neck. I couldn't scream anymore. My throat was too sore, and vomit kept coming out, leaving me helpless. I didn't under-stand such violence. Why? My eyes focused on the man that was now on the ground next to the girl he killed. I memo-rized him too. I trembled as I tried to move but whimpered.

Dread sunk in as my stomach began to burn—I'm going to die here.

I whimpered and begged my mother to answer me. The blackness in my vision kept lulling me toward sleep. I closed my eyes and I saw the man's pure thrill of satisfaction as he snapped the girl's neck. Although I fought to stay awake, to grab my mother's cellphone to call the police, the blackness pulled me under.

"Clear!"

"Clear!"

I woke to the sound of people bustling about. Sirens blaring. Then silence rained down on the entire commotion.

"DOA," someone I couldn't see said. What did that mean? I tried to get back to Momma, but the blackness kept clawing at me.

"Momma?" I screamed as I woke up with a gasp. Disorientation buried itself deep down inside of me. Scared, I called for her again, this time louder. Still no answer. No, instead, a woman in a green uniform came over to me.

"Shh, it's going to be all right. Everything is going to be all right." I looked at the woman as hot tears ran down my face. Two more people entered the room. One was a stern looking woman. The other was a doctor. She had to be, her white coat said so. She was frowning at the other woman.

"Charlotte Camilio?" the stern looking woman asked, opening her notepad and clicking a pen in her left hand. I nodded but I couldn't make eye contact with her. The doctor huffed and the nurse stroked my hair out of my face.

"I'm Officer Torrez." She paused, probably to make sure I was paying attention. "I need you to tell me everything that you remember." Her demand was forceful enough to make my stomach roll. The world began to tilt, and I couldn't breathe. As the nurse put a cool cloth over my throat to calm me down, I shook. Fear made me tremble as the memory began to invade my consciousness. I began to cry.

"I told you, she is not ready to talk. Dammit, now, if you have more questions, you are going to have to wait to ask them," the doctor snapped in my defense. I closed my eyes as the officer began to bicker with the doctor. Her voice grated my nerves. Making me sick. I know she didn't mean to, but I was frantic for her to leave.

"I know nothing. All I remember is the car came toward us and then we began to flip." I closed my eyes and shuddered. A loud huff sounded as the woman made her way out of the room. I had lied to her. I knew everything that happened, but I couldn't tell anyone. No, those men were dangerous. My mind shut down and I fell back to sleep.

As my consciousness stirred back to life, I noticed a young man sitting to the right of the bed. "Ah, you are awake. Wonderful. I'm David Smith. You can call me Haydes. Everyone does. I'm your social worker." He smiled at me, and I noted how warm and kind it was as it stretched across his face. I felt safe with him. I somehow just knew I could trust him. I didn't feel that way about Officer Torrez. I knew it didn't make sense. She was a police officer and trustworthy, right? I looked at Haydes, concerned.

"Why do I need a social worker?" My mind wasn't grasping why he would be here.

"I'm here to find you a new family." He looked down and straightened an invisible part of his clothing. His eyes, as he stared up at me, burned bright. I could now tell why his name was Haydes.

"I don't need a new family. I already have one. Momma and I were going on a trip. She is in the room next door." She had to be. There was no way Momma would ever leave me alone. Not like this. And since I was in the hospital, she had to be here with me. She had to be.

Haydes looked down and sighed. He came over and sat down on the bed. He grabbed one of my hands and made me focus on him. "Charlotte ..."

I didn't let him finish. "What's going on? Where's my mother?"

Two

KRONOS

Ten Years Earlier

"HAPPY BIRTHDAY, BABY," the drunk ass girl in the passenger seat said. Our car went barreling down the highway. She stroked my thigh as my youngest stepbrother, Ayres, had his tongue deep down a woman's throat. The moans were loud, but I didn't pay attention to the noise. No, I looked at the girl, the one whose name I couldn't remember, "Get your dirty mouth on my cock, right now."

She didn't move fast enough so I pulled her head toward me as she took her seat belt off. I laughed at the fact that it was so easy to pick up free pussy. Her hands unzipped my jeans and my hard cock thanked her by springing out between the zipper teeth. She took me in her mouth and before I knew it, she had me down her throat—balls deep. Damn, if I were one to keep girls around, I would have kept her just to give me head when I needed it.

The sound of crunching metal and screams forced my eyes

open. *Fuck, when did I close my eyes?* I looked and saw the car in front us flipping over. The young girl inside was screaming for help and looked right at me. Her gaze never faltered as they tumbled over another three times. The first inkling of guilt set in. I didn't have time to process it.

The driver was dead. I could tell by the bones sticking out of her neck and the dead stare. The young girl kept screaming as the car came to a stop upside down. She was stuck. But then again, so was I. Somewhere between awe in the fact that she dared to stare me down—and confusion on how I hit the damn car.

"Kr ... Kronos," Ayres croaked.

"Yeah, I'm alive."

Paying attention to the girl that was still in my lap, I wondered what her name was. As I shook her, the steering wheel squeezed deeper into her neck. Yeah, she wasn't alive anymore. I could have pulled away. But hell, I'm a sick bastard. I pumped five times into her mouth and came down her throat. I have to say, I smiled as I watched the cum seeping out of her broken neck and onto the steering wheel. Fuck, I could go again. One more time. I smiled and brought her head up and down on my cock. That's until I heard Ayres cussing up a storm and the back door creaking open.

"My leg, it's broken, and this bitch weighs a fucking ton," he growled as he threw her out of the car. She was alive. Damn, with the way she was carrying on in his lap, she shouldn't be in the car. Ayres' hold must have been hard on her. I heard him fall out of the car and I disengaged the girl from my cock. Zipping up my pants, I slid from the front seat. Stretching, I thought about what I needed to do. It was going to be a long night.

My thoughts went to how to clean the mess up. Watching Ayres, he sat down on the ground next to the girl and broke her neck. Her gurgling was a turn on and I had to straighten my junk. At least Ayres was merciful, that time. He didn't toy with killing her.

He crawled to the curb as I pulled the plates from the car. Going around the front of the car, I took the plates there and scratched the VIN number out on both the door and the dash. No reason to leave a trace of who we are. Pulling the gun from the glove compartment, the thought of killing the girl in the other car came to my mind.

Turning around, I saw that she had fainted. Blood was seeping from her stomach. I holstered the gun. She would be dead within a matter of minutes. No point in wasting a bullet. Opening the trunk, I pulled out the gasoline and poured it all over the car. I hated to see the brand-new Escalade going up in flames, but hell, it was better than a trace back to us.

"She's still alive," Ayres groaned, looking at the girl in the other car. Looking back, I dialed our other stepbrother, Hypnos. I ignored Ayres as Hypnos answered after the fourth ring. It was quite hard to hear him, music was thumping in the background.

"Come get us," I demanded in the lowest voice I could as I watched the girl that had been giving me head catch fire. My hard-on was back. Fuck me. I picked up the other dead girl and threw her back in the car. "Might as well leave no witnesses." I laughed as Ayres smirked.

"What about the other car?"

"They are both dead anyways."

Taking Ayres in my arms, I hoisted him over my shoulder. We walked away from the scene as the distant roar of sirens blared. Someone must have heard the wreck and called it in. There was no one outside, so I knew it was safe enough to keep going. I sure as fuck didn't call the cops. It was the girl. I smirked at the thought of her having such gumption. She stared me down even in her frightened state. She must have grabbed her mother's phone.

I helped Ayres stand as Hypnos pulled up. The shit head only made us walk three blocks.

"About fucking time Hypnos," Ayres complained while I laughed.

"Get in, shut up and let's go get that leg set."

Hypnos looked at us both, shaking his head as he put his SUV into gear. No more thinking about the girl that was bleeding out in the middle of the worst car accident I had ever seen.

————

WE GOT TO OUR FAMILY HOME AND OUR DOCTOR MET US there. After taking one of the painkillers he gave me, I went to bed, not thinking anything about what happened. It was better that way or I would obsess over the girl.

My phone ringing startled me from sleep. "What?" I demanded as I answered the phone. Looking at the clock, I realized it was three in the morning. "This better be good to be calling me now, at this hour."

"Kronos, it's Officer Torrez. I found one of your cars out on Route 2." Chills ran down my spine as the officer carried on, talking about how she knew it was me that left that wreck. I denied it all. As we're taught to do.

"By the way, the girl, she's alive, and she knows nothing."

Three

CHARLOTTE

Present Day

DEEP BREATH, I tell myself again for what seems like the tenth time. You can do this. My little pep talk isn't working. Then again, nothing could stop me from going through with this. Hand on the door, I close my eyes.

Deep breath.

I walk into the tattoo parlor and spot my best friend, Amy Diggerson. She smiles at me, and I meet her halfway for a hug. "I'm glad you finished your shift. Come on, we'll get started."

Taking off my coat, I sit on her swivel stool. "Amy, I'm still nervous about this."

"Good. If you weren't, you wouldn't be ready. Everyone gets nervous before a tattoo. Let me show you the sketch and if you don't like it, we won't go forward tonight."

This makes me feel better. Wringing my hands in my lap, I wait for the sketch. *What if I hate it?* I don't have to wait long because the moment she shows me the drawing, I fall in love.

"Oh, yes. This is perfect." Amy winks at me and my nerves begin to dissipate. "This will be the perfect homage to my mom." The tattoo is a small dove sitting on a cherry blossom branch.

"See, I told you. Now get comfortable. We're going to be here for at least two hours."

As the needle moves around my tender skin, the memory hits me. My sweet mother, gone in the blink of an eye. The pain in my heart overtakes the pain in my shoulder. Sniffling, I close my eyes, trying to stay within the present and not get stuck in the past. Stuck on the man's eyes that still haunt my dreams.

"Sweetie, I know this is hard. But you've come so far. One more sweep across the tail and then we're finished."

I know that Amy assumes I'm thinking about the tattoo and how it's hurting. But I'm not. "All right." I clear my throat and think about how Amy has always been such a good friend. I've known her for the last year. If I hadn't switched my chemistry lab, I wouldn't have her as a friend. She hates science but I was able to help her through our labs.

Cold cream hits my skin and I blink away my wayward thoughts. "The tattoo is all done. Here, look." She turns a mirror around so I can see her work. Tears well in my eyes, and I nod.

"It's perfect."

After another round of hugs, Amy ushers me outside, telling me to get home as quickly as possible. The wind whips my hair about as I zip up my coat. I shiver and wonder why the air is so crisp. I tremble as my stomach rumbles, signaling I need to eat. As the wind picks up once again, I curse myself for not having a car or a cellphone.

It'd be nice to call an Uber. Five more blocks, I tell myself. My stomach is not having it though. Huffing in agitation, I walk into the 24-hour gas station on the worst corner of the neighborhood. Pulling out my money, I become disheartened. Five dollars. Five stinking dollars. Oh well, a bag of chips and a candy bar will have to do.

"Hey Eddie." The clerk that is always reading magazines and chewing tobacco looks up at me. His face lights up as he puts his magazine down and spits into his cup.

"Charlotte, good to see you, sugar." I chuckle and stop to talk to him, asking him about his wife. He chats with me for quite a bit before going back to his magazine. I smile and look at the food as my stomach rumbles.

"Put your money away, sugar. Get you some food, it's on the house." I smile at Eddie, as heat warms my cheeks.

"Thank you, Eddie."

I try not to think about the fact that Eddie gives me free food once a week or so. I go around the store picking out food that could last up to a week. I don't want him to think I'm taking advantage. I don't have a car, so I'm stuck between Sandy's Bar, this gas station, and my apartment on most days. I have my items in hand when a commotion happens at the front of the store.

Yelling ensues and my heart rate goes wild inside of my chest. I try to relax but as the mean voices continue, I hide behind a drink display.

"Where's our money, Eddie?"

What money? Is Eddie in trouble? I stop myself. What am I doing? I stand up and make my way toward the front. The cocking of a gun makes me stop dead in my tracks.

"Eddie, you have to the count of three to give us what we're owed or I'm going to put a bullet in that old noggin of yours. Do you understand me?"

Eddies' old voice cracks, and as he speaks, he looks right at me. His eyes bulge from his head as his pupils grow large. My breathing intensifies as he looks at me and glances toward the back of the store, pleading with me to run and hide. I duck right back down behind the drink display. "Here's your money, now get out."

I'm able to see the guys in the mirrored glass of the drink cases. The one on the left has on a wife beater, blue jeans, and a pair of black boots. Tattoos line his arms. Dear me, he looks like a god. Black hair with silver in it. I can remember that. I have a photographic memory, so I know I'll remember all of this forever. The middle one—I blink in shock—he has on a three-piece tailored suit. My eyes roam over him, landing on his auburn locks and clean skin—a complete contrast to the first man. *Got it.* My attention lands on the third man, scanning over his black cargo pants and dark hoodie. Three quite different men, yet they're together. I commit everything to memory and know I'll be able to help Eddie as soon as they're gone.

As I'm in my head, the door chimes and I look up as Eddie stands over me. He reaches out a hand and I grab it. "What... what's going on Eddie?"

Eddie helps me up, sighing, unable to look at me with his swollen eyes. "Those are the Power's Brothers. They own this side of town. You see them by yourself, you run. Run as fast as you can. Do you understand me?"

I nod. "Good, now let's get you out of here."

"Eddie, we need to call the police. I'm sorry I don't have a cellphone, or I would have already done it." He starts laughing, hard.

"No police, sugar. They own the police on this side of town as well. You live, what, two blocks? Get home. Straight home. Make no stops."

He puts my items in a bag and I leave, my heart feeling strange. My mind races as I start my journey home. We should have called the police anyway. What if they're going to do worse things? Why were they demanding money? My mind spins too fast for me to process everything as I open a bottle of water and try to calm my nerves.

Sandy's Bar comes into view, and I smile. They're busy for a Wednesday night. Sandy's Bar marks the one block mark for me. Now I must pass the old newspaper office on the right and then turn the corner. I hate walking past the newspaper office. It stinks so bad. Squatters are always in there, doing god knows what. Taking a deep breath, I book it past the place and as soon as I turn the corner, I let my breath out, breathing a little easier.

The biggest obstacle though, is Dead Man's Alley. The air around Dead Man's Alley screams out into the night. This place churns my stomach. It's the only way to the apartment and if I keep my head down, I will make it. "Keep walking," I repeat continuously to myself.

My ears perk up at what sounds like a scuffle. Angry voices. Sobbing. The sound of something wet splattering on the ground. My back hits the wall of the building I was passing. "Don't look Charlotte. Don't look."

Curiosity seeps into my brain. Before I can tell myself not to look again, I step around the building and freeze. A man is standing above two bodies on the ground—baseball bat in hand, laughing like a maniac. Fear grips me as I watch the man bring the bat down, hitting the body closest to him. He turns, bringing the bat again toward the other body. The sound of the baseball bat hitting the bodies echoes in my brain as my lower lip trembles. This cannot be happening.

"No," the word comes from somewhere a little deeper in the alley. I peel my eyes away from the grotesque scene to stare at the other two men that had been in the store. The guy with the wife beater on, holds a sobbing woman in his arms. His hands squeeze tightly around her throat as she struggles to yank free from his grip. My heart cracks in my chest as I choke back my own sobs for the woman. Her high heels scrape across the asphalt as I try to focus on the scene taking place right in front of me.

The man in the suit from the gas station brings down a knife and guts the man right in front of everyone. I watch the knife come down, one, two, three, four times. I am stuck here, watching the man whisper to the woman, "I love you," as he slumps down to the ground. I should be running. Instead, my hands begin to shake and the bag I was holding drops. I gasp and four sets of eyes turn my way. I stand, dumbfounded at the carnage. Shock. That's what has a hold of me. *Shock.*

The woman's neck breaks with an ease that terrifies me. My mind flashes back to the car accident—to the way the man on the ground broke the girl's neck—and a sob pours from my throat as I flee the scene. I cannot believe I saw this. I cannot ... No, I have to get home. I can't stop at the police department. I told Eddie I would get home. I run as fast as I can.

"Fuck," the word rings out into the night as an eerie promise. "Stop her. No fucking witnesses." I knew these three would be trouble.

And if they catch me, I'm as good as dead.

◆

Four

AYRES

Skittish little kitten ran before I got to see her. My brother's outburst made me look up from my pleasure task. Yeah, I was masturbating over the fuckers I beat to death. Sue me. I get horny when I see blood. The sweet sound of bones giving way makes me think of moans in the heat of the moment.

Nostrils flared; Kronos looks like a bull ready to charge. *No witnesses*, it's his rule. He means it, too. I zip my hard as a rock cock back into my pants with a grunt. Putting my bat in the holder on my back, I take off running. I'm quite sure she didn't run back toward the gas station. But she came from that way and the sack on the ground tells me she was in that store. That means the old man either knows her—or has a video of her. He better tell me what he knows. I grin at that thought, because if he doesn't, I get to beat the ever-loving shit out of him.

As I get closer to the store, I look down at my pants, laughing. Blood is splattered like red paint all over me. Oh well. It will help drill my point home. When I walk through the door, I realize another guest is in the store. A beautiful young woman who looks like a motorcycle club stripper.

"Amy, you need to go."

"Oh, now Eddie, let her stay. She can help me with this hard on." The woman sucks in a breath. I chuckle with a dark glee in my eyes.

"Ayres, let the lady leave." I stop in my tracks. This is the first time that Eddie has stood up to me. I like it. It means I'm going to get to have fun now.

"No. We are going to have a little chat." I bring my baseball bat out and slap it across the counter. This causes both Eddie and the woman to back away from me. Cat and mouse. I laugh with an evil thought. *Cat and mouse, baby.*

"Please," the woman begs me. Fucking music to my ears. I grab her head and pull her to me as she yelps.

"I said no. Now get on your knees." Eddie protests and I push the woman down on her knees. She trembles and whimpers.

"Please!" she says, trying to beg for her freedom. "Pl—"

"Shut up, both of you. Now Eddie, unless I give you permission to speak, this bitch is going to suck my cock. Unless you give me the answers I want, that is."

The beautiful woman is crying now. Her mascara streaks thick, dark, inky lines down her cheeks. Eddie slaps his hand down on the counter and I smirk at his boldness.

"Now Eddie, the girl that was in here before this sweet ass came in, who is she?"

Eddie looks at me. His wheels are turning, I can already tell he's trying to evade my question. I shove my cock down the girl's throat. She chokes at first and then the bitch tries to bite down. I moan.

"Oh, sweet slut, I love a good bite. You need to bite harder."

She looks up at me, her eyes wide—like I took her by surprise. I wink at her.

"Ayres, stop," the old man begs. I won't stop, though. Instead, I thrust my hips into her face. She's choking, slobber running down the front of my pants and her chin.

"The faster you give me a name, the faster I'm out of here."

Thrust.

Grunt.

Thrust.

The girl chokes out a sob as I chuckle, rolling my head back because I'm so fucking close. The sweet release I need is building, my core muscles tighten and the old, familiar feeling creeps in as she cries on my cock. The girl's mouth is nice, but she's sobbing too much. She isn't supplying enough suction. She tries to pull away from me and I yank her hair. This forces her head all the way down on my cock. She tries to push my legs and I slap her face with brutal force.

"Stop moving or I'll kill you right now."

"I don't know her name. She comes in here from Sandy's bar and goes toward the newspaper office when she leaves. That's all I know." He isn't telling me the whole truth, the old man wants to play games.

My rage flies through the roof and I glare at him. "Oh Eddie. You shouldn't have lied."

Without a second thought, I snap the girl's neck. Gurgling noises leave her throat as her lifeless body hits the floor. I turn to Eddie as cum drips out of the woman's lips—my cum. Only the counter separates Eddie and I and he hunches over, his breath coming in short, ragged bursts as he tries to control it. I imagine this is his first time to ever see a murder. Too bad for him it will be his last, though.

"Eddie ... Eddie ... Eddie ... What's her name?"

He stares at the woman as his face crumples, falling into a jagged expression. "Rose. Her name is Rose." Nodding, I pull the bat back and slap it across Eddie's face. The sound of his face breaking fills the silent gas station.

"Thank you." Jumping across the counter, I bring my bat down against his stomach. He grunts. Ah, he's still alive. So, satisfying to hear. He mumbles for me to stop but I ignore him. I bring the bat down again and this time it's against his manhood. He howls and I snicker. "We're just getting started, Eddie."

His eyes close and I'm having such a fun time. I look at the camera behind where Eddie had been standing. *Perfect.* I bring the bat down again against his skull and he takes his last breath. He's broken. Brain dead. Lifeless. That's two more people dead tonight. I take the girl's purse and cell phone before I pull the tapes from the shelf and the one that is in the VCR. Without so much as a backward glance, I leave the store. The girl, Rose, will be dead before we go home tonight. Sending a text to Kronos, I tell him the girl's name is Rose and she frequents the bar on this street. I let him know I have the tapes as well.

I dump the girl's purse in a nearby dumpster after I take her wallet. The girl had money. She sure did dress like a hooker. But the way she sucked dick told me she wasn't a professional. My phone rings as I step back into Dead Man's Alley.

"Rose is not her name. Sandy confirmed she doesn't have anyone by that name there. Go back to Eddie and see what we can find."

"Eddie's dead."

"Dammit, Ayres. Fine, burn the bodies in the alley. Hypnos and I will be around the corner soon enough for Eddie," he grunts out.

Before he hangs up I quickly say, "There's a dead girl in the store, too." He ends the call with a sigh before I can say anything else. Shrugging my shoulders, I whistle the tune, "Monster" by Meg Meyers. I stack the bodies together in a huddle. These jackasses deserved their deaths tonight. They owed us money and when they refused to pay, they signed their death warrants. It was a shame I didn't get to play with them longer. Reaching into my pocket, I pull out my lighter. The feeling of exhilaration hits me as I light them up. It doesn't take long for their bodies to become engulfed.

I readjust myself. Most people would gag at the smell of burning flesh but not me. No, it has the opposite effect. "Shit," I moan and readjust once again.

"The buildings are empty," Hypnos announces as he walks up, tossing Eddie onto the pile.

"We can't be chasing a ghost. Eddie said her name was Rose. Kronos didn't find her at Sandy's Bar. So here, these are the tapes from the station. If we don't find her, we can figure it out once we get home."

Hypnos shifts, trying to hide his disgust for the smell that's permeating the chilly night air. Kronos comes up with the girl and I smile. Her mouth is stuck in an O shape. So damn sexy. My dick is hard as a rock again. Damn, I need to get laid.

"There's an apartment building down about three blocks. Hypnos said he saw a girl enter a building right next to it but didn't find anything. I say we go to the apartment building and we torture everyone in there to get answers. We don't get answers, we torch the place," Kronos growls as he looks at the burning bodies.

"Ayres was able to get the tapes. We can watch them back at the gas station if you want?" Hypnos speaks up, trying to calm Kronos.

"No. We have to hunt this girl down. Now." Kronos looks

at both of us. "What, just because we have tapes doesn't mean we are going to get a damn thing, this ends tonight."

His words are final. Hypnos nods his understanding and I follow suit. I can't help but pop off. "Before we kill her, I'm tapping that ass."

Five

CHARLOTTE

Anxiety threatens to take over my mind as I sprint into the street, wondering where I'm going to go. If I run to the bar, they'll follow me. Hell, I can't bring my drama to Sandy's. My mind races. The thought of dying tonight makes my stomach quiver. The scar along my stomach aches—letting me know danger is near. I mean, who else has a bat signal for danger? Me. I do. And I listen to my gut. Always.

"No way I'm dying tonight," I whisper to myself. I dash into the abandoned building to the right of my apartment building. It's two buildings wide. There's an underground passage to my apartment building that should give me cover. I hope. The men make no attempt to be quiet. I guess their plan is made. I hear two pairs of feet hitting the pavement, fading.

I stand here on the filth of the building for a moment. "Oh, God." The man cusses, fumbling through the trash at the entrance. This place is a loitering hole for miscreants. They leave everything and anything behind. I try not to think about what might be crawling all over me.

"Come out now. We only want to talk." The tone in which the man speaks tells me talking is the last thing they have in mind for me. I take a deep breath and leap into action. I know where this building leads, and the man doesn't. I remember the path from this building to my apartment complex. When I moved here, I found the exits. The hiding spots. The dead ends and the traps. I never moved to a new spot without developing an escape plan. Shit hit the fan way too often to be naive enough to think I didn't need to know how to get out of a jam.

The man is behind me, angry. I have to be quiet but that's quite hard to do with all this trash around. As quiet as I can be, I make my way to the staircase. Underneath the staircase is a door that's hidden in plain sight. You have to know where to push on the wall to get it to open. As the door opens, I hear the man cuss. He's already upstairs. I make a mental note that the man is impatient. Or stupid, not to follow the path I had. It didn't matter. I have to get out of here.

The man is opening doors now. He isn't very subtle, not even trying to be quiet. I close the door, thinking about how this man is hunting me. Ready to kill me. My stomach knots itself and I gasp, overwhelmed. I make my way through the tunnel, thinking about how I'm going to have to burn these clothes. To move. *Again.* I focus on not thinking about what I've seen tonight. The stabbing of the man. The beating of the dead corpses. The ease of the man snapping that woman's neck. I'm going to be sick, but I have to steel myself.

The sound of noises in the tunnel freaks me out. I run all the way to the door that leads me home. I have to believe they don't know where I live. They don't know my name. And if I'm lucky, they didn't get a good look at me. They won't find me. I'll call Haydes and ask for another favor in finding a new place closer to the college. That is, if Haydes answers me. He's been kind of radio silent since I started working and moved to the south side of Timberland.

"Hey girlie, you got any spare change?" I almost simultaneously scream and throw up in my mouth, looking at the old lady from room 104. Her teeth are molding, and warts cover her skin. I smile, trying to be a better person than my mind is.

"I'm sorry, no. Have a good night." I whisper as I maneuver around her. I race up the last flight of stairs and sigh. My hands shake so badly, I can't keep from fumbling with the keys. I'm able to calm down enough to unlock the door, get in and shut the outside world out. I have to think positive. First thing first though, I need to take a shower. Then I'll make my call. Ripping the clothes off my body, I shove them into the garbage can, tears running down my face. I know I have to be quick and quiet.

Locking my bedroom door, I make a beeline for the shower and jump in. The cold hits me and I tremble, but it's better than standing in my bathroom naked. My life has officially changed forever, and the water isn't washing it away. I scrub hard and fast. Then slow and hard. Nothing makes me feel clean enough. After the third time washing, I finally start to wash my hair, thinking of how I need Haydes.

"I sure hope he is going to answer his phone," I whisper into the steam.

Six

HYPNOS

AYRES WATCHES the bodies burn as I stand by, looking over the area. Kronos paces, probably wondering what the fuck is going on. A small sound comes from above. "There," I say, pointing to the third floor of the apartment building behind us, "we got her." Kronos smirks as he looks up, "Kill them all." Ayres comes around the corner just as the gas station blows up. "Just like clockwork boys." Ayres starts laughing like crazy. He's such a child sometimes.

Kronos rolls his eyes and growls, "Shut up. The police will be here within minutes. The fire department right after them. We have a hunch the girl is in the apartments on the third floor. Now be quiet so we can go into the building and kill her."

Ayres quiets down and I pull out my knife. I shouldn't be excited about the idea of getting to carve the bitch up, but I am. My chest swells with giddiness. We walk into the dilapidated building and Kronos heads to the second floor. Ayres will work on clearing the third floor—but he's been instructed not to touch the far east apartment. I'll be clearing the first floor. I come across an old man first. I smile and slit his throat. Before I move on to help Kronos, I hear moaning coming from the far back apartment.

A sadistic feeling washes over me and Kronos's words hit me once again. *Kill them all.* I bust into the apartment. The couple on the couch doesn't even flinch. The woman is on her knees, blissed out. I can tell right away because the man she's sucking off has her head down on him past what's normal for any human. Yet, she's here, sucking away. The man grins a silly grin.

"Wanna join?" he asks in that sweet voice that only someone high can achieve, especially when an intruder bursts into one's apartment.

"Sure," I wink and then throw my knife, hitting him straight in his left eye. A small gurgle comes from him as the light visibly dims in his right eye. The girl never stops sucking. Fucking junkies. I push the girl's head down. She doesn't even gag and I chuckle.

"Good girl." She gives me a side eye. Submission written all over her face. I almost don't go through with it, but then I slice her throat and watch her blood flow down on the cock she was just sucking.

"Mm." The moan slips out of my mouth. I love seeing the blood flow. My adrenaline rushes through my veins as I pick the girl up and drape her around the couch. My dick is throbbing, and well, an easy pussy is always nice. Unzipping my pants, I shove my cock into her not-so-tight pussy.

"Fucking whore," I think as I slack my hunger into her. As I come, I feel sick. I'll have to take a Lye soap bath when I get home. Walking out, Kronos glares at me from the second floor as I adjust my pants, sticking my dick back in them.

I chuckle and climb the stairs. "Let's do this," Ayres says as we get to the third floor. We walk down to the apartment and try the door. It has a flimsy lock that's rusted on the outside. The smell of sugar and cinnamon hits me hard. My cock grows hard in an instant. I can't believe it.

"Fuck," Kronos whispers. He adjusts himself and Ayres brings the baseball bat down, looking stricken. We push into the room as the girl comes out of her bathroom and freezes. Terror running along her features. Her eyes well with tears, but she has a fire about her. I can feel it.

"Just..." Her voice falters and I shift. My dick throbbing. I'm not sure I can move. The most innocent, beautiful angel is standing right before us.

Seven

CHARLOTTE

No. They can't be here. My heart races. My world crumbles as I look at the trio. This... this is my worst nightmare standing before me. I ramble in my brain, and nothing comes out of my mouth. Not one word. The man with the bloody knife steps forward.

"Just get out. I saw nothing. I know nothing. Please. Just leave." My voice is weak. I'm shaking like a leaf. I can't believe I'm still standing. One more step. The man is getting too close.

"Stop. Not a..." The baseball bat guy chuckles, and I look at him. Chucking my brush at the knife guy, I run into my bedroom, slamming the door and locking it.

"Feisty Little Warrior," he chuckles. I can hear him. Oh, God. What do I do? I look around my room and run to the window and toward the fire escape. I can run from there. I know I can. The door busts into a million pieces as I climb through the window.

"Get her!" A voice calls out as I run down the first flight of stairs, the wind and chill cutting through me. Before I can get to the bottom a large body drops on me. I bang my knees on the steel stairs and cry out as the man pins me.

"Oh, Little Warrior," the man says as he grinds his erection into my ass. I freeze. "The things I'm going to do to you."

I have one arm free, and I jam it backwards, right into his face. His grip on me loosens as he gasps for air. I'm able to slip out from under him but run straight into another wall of a man.

"Oh, Kitten. You are a beauty," the man chuckles into a purr. He has me in a bear hug. "You are caught. Give it up little one."

I growl with determination, stomping on his foot. Just as I'm about to stick my knee in his groin, a gun cocks and I realize it's pointing right at my head.

"Enough." The demand comes sternly. "You don't hold any power here. You are surrounded and only alive right now because..."

The one with the knife cuts in, "Because we want to fuck you."

I blush brightly. God he's so crass. I take a deep breath. "No. Kill me now, you bastards." I begin to fight even more. I must have taken the guy by surprise because he looks at me with a wide-open mouth and then slaps me. Hard.

I cry out in shock. "Damn little kitten has claws," he says as he rubs his cheek where I had clawed him. The man with the gun pushes me against the wall of the apartment building. I'm terrified. My adrenaline is fading fast. The gun presses into my chin. Eyes wide, I stare at the man. His bold angry eyes. Those green eyes make me stop. My entire body shakes as flashbacks drum into me—the night my mother died. It all comes flooding back like a nightmare. Those same eyes stare at me all over again as he stands nose to nose with me.

"If I must, I will blow your brains out. But you can live tonight. You don't settle down though, your life is over. "

He slips his tongue into my mouth. My first kiss, stolen. He tastes like whiskey and sin. I tremble as tears run down my face. This is not good. In fact, this is the exact opposite. This is bad. So, so bad. His lips demand that I open, give in to him. I whimper into his mouth and try to pull back. I really don't want to kiss him. He gives me no choice.

"Fuck, look at her body squirm. Come on dude, let's get out of here before we fuck her right here and get caught by the police."

This clears the fog of the man kissing me. "You are pigs." I scoff and spit at the man that had just stolen something I could never get back. Had I known that he was going to do worse, I would have let him continue to kiss me.

"Good little rabbit." The words come right before he cold cocks me with the butt of his gun. I look at him, dazed, and my world goes twirling into blackness.

"No..." I gasp as my head knocks backward. The last thing I remember is pleading, "No..."

Eight

KRONOS

Her lips felt so good against mine. She dared to look me in the eyes. *Bold.* Such a bold little rabbit. As she slumps down, Hypnos picks her up.

"She's just one little girl and she's given us more of a fight than anyone we've come across in almost a decade." Ayres shakes his head as we go down the last flight of stairs. I open the door to the SUV and get in the passenger seat.

"This is a God damn issue. I should have put a bullet in her skull." Hypnos drops her onto the backseat as Ayres starts the engine.

"Oh, shut up. The best damn thing we can do is use her up. We are going to enjoy that young pussy."

Hypnos laughs. "Yeah, very nice young pussy." He runs a hand along her thigh. Her creamy, untarnished thigh. My cock begins to pulse, and I have to adjust before I get a zipper imprint on it.

"Strip her naked Hypnos." I want to see those perky little tits. I bet those nipples are a soft pink. A blush waiting for us to enjoy. Ayres speeds away just as I hit the button on my phone. The apartment building catches on fire, the explosion making us swerve. I smirk. The police officers and firefighters come barreling down the street, speeding past us.

I watch as Hypnos takes off the girl's panties. He shoves them into her mouth and begins to slap her thighs. It doesn't rouse her. If it weren't for her little mumbling, I would have thought I had killed her.

"Cinnamon." The sound of ecstasy coming from Hypnos is starting to make me want something hardcore.

"Tie her up. She can wake up and start fighting again. We don't need that right now," I state the obvious. I watch as he strips her down. I was right. Fuck me, I was right. Those little nipples are the color of a blushing rose.

"Fuck." The moan floats out of me before I can stop myself. Hypnos flicks her left nipple and then squeezes it. She moans as he ties her hands to the door. Before I can say anything, he pushes her legs up and ties them to her arms. Her soft pussy is open for the taking. Hypnos touches her and this time, she comes alive.

We watch as she yanks, her eyes opening. I can tell the moment she realizes her predicament. Her body goes rigid. Those long legs start pulling and moving but she's going nowhere fast.

"Stop straining, little rabbit. It's going to be worse if you keep this up."

She turns to me and dares to look at me. *Again.* Such a bold rabbit. "Hypnos, play with her pussy. Let's see if she is as innocent as she looks."

Hypnos is all too happy to play with her. He touches her clit and she jolts, writhing against him. She tries to move away from him but all that does is slip his finger lower. Hypnos laughs and I smile. "Press a finger in her. Tell us how tight she is."

Her head starts moving back and forth in a *no* fashion. "That's it, Little Warrior. Enjoying that aren't you?" Hypnos coos at her. She's trying to fight it. But we can see it. The hitch of her breath. The hardening of her nipples and that sweet body is shaking. She's fighting it. No matter what though, her body is enjoying it and there's no hiding that.

He tries to shove a finger into her pussy. It barely goes in. I can't believe it. "Holy fuck. She..." He looks at me and Ayres looks back at him just as I did.

"She what?" we both ask at the same time.

"My finger isn't going all the way in. She's tight. This sweet little thing..." he pauses. "She's a virgin." My ears can't believe it, can't latch onto what he's saying. But the way she's crying— well, bawling—tells us it's true. She wiggles. She yanks. She tries her damnedest to stop Hypnos from moving his fingers into her but it doesn't work. Hypnos tries inching slowly and methodically into her pussy. One finger, back and forth. She closes her eyes, mortification written all over her sweet, tear-streaked face.

Ayres swerves and I slap him on the head. "Watch the road. You'll get your turn with her soon enough."

Nine

CHARLOTTE

HYPNOS. That's the man's name. I try to move away from him as he continues trying to force his way into my untouched body. He grabs his knife and nicks me against my right breast and I gasp from the sheer pain. He cut me. Air hits the newly formed slice on my skin and I hiss in pain. I tremble. This is absolutely the worst-case scenario I've always tried to steer clear of, even when I was younger.

"Be still. Or don't." He shrugs. "I can do this all damn night." He narrows his eyes, growling at me. I'm naked, it's the first time I've ever been naked in front of anyone and I'm in front of three men. My face flames with embarrassment. Not only am I naked in front of them but I'm being touched on top of it. I can't find a way out of this moment. It might be the worst thing about this entire situation—feeling helpless. My mind races and I can't control it. The more he tries to take my body, the feeling of hope dissipates, and agony fills me.

He shoves in once again, and my traitorous body opens for him. *No. No.* I know they can't hear me. But this... it isn't what I want, not by a long shot. I move and his finger goes a little deeper. Tears run down my face as my body loses control to this man. I can't stop it, can't fight it, but at the same time I do not want this to be how I lose my virginity. Or how I die.

"Let me taste," the man in the passenger seat grits out and I close my eyes. I don't think I can handle this. This is above what I can comprehend. I open my eyes just as the man offers his finger to the other man. They both moan and I blink in shock. I don't understand why my body is tingling. I am so hot and so scared at the same time. Everything in my mind is jumbled up and I can't control the rapid beating of my heart, my pulse thumping in my temples.

"Pull over Ayres."

The car swerves again as the man pulls over. The lights are blinding. The sound of people fills the air around us. I can't see much, but the bright lights and scent of gasoline filling my nostrils tell me we must be at a gas station.

"Help!" I try to scream but it doesn't do one bit of good. My mouth is full of something—my words mumbled. No one is coming to help me.

The man, Hypnos, leans his massive body over mine, putting the knife to my throat. I blink at him before scrunching my eyes closed. "Move again. I dare you. Because if you do, you're dead."

I freeze. There's no way I want to die. The car doors open and Ayres, the driver, stands before me. He unties my hands and legs from the door and I struggle to keep from being tied up again. The man grabs my hands and places them against my stomach, wrapping rope around my waist to keep them in place. Hypnos puts the knife away as he holds my legs. I kick at him, and he just laughs. "Feisty little warrior."

Ayres chuckles. "Oh yeah," he says with an evil smirk. The sound of his zipper coming down makes me bawl even harder.

"Don't do this. Please." I'm bawling so much I choke on my words. My body is shaking in fear. My stomach edges its way into my throat. I can't breathe. I'm on the verge of a panic attack.

"Kronos let's tape this," Hypnos says as he moves his finger in and out of my now wet pussy. My eyes go wide. *Tape...* tape it? *No, please.*

Shaking my head, I refuse. This cannot be happening. "No... No..." Ayres doesn't let me continue to talk. He stuffs his hard cock into my mouth. I sputter trying to move away from him. My head is going nowhere. With the way Ayres has pulled the door open, it makes my head hang off the seat. I can't move at all now. He holds onto my neck, forcing himself down my throat.

"Open that mouth," Ayres growls at me. I don't obey his command. He slaps both my breasts and then pulls my nipples. I scream and it's the perfect timing for Ayres. He's able to shove in and out of my mouth with ease now. I choke but even that doesn't stop him.

"Fuck yeah," he moans. He holds my head as he drives in and out of my mouth. Hypnos lays an arm along my legs and continues playing with my pussy. He flicks my clit and then shoves his finger into my folds, making me uneasy at the feeling growing inside of me.

Kronos sits on his knees in the front seat, his phone in front of him—he really is taping this. He is taping these men, taping them when they are about to violate me...and he's enjoying it. Ayres pushes my face straight into his balls and growls, "Do it Hypnos. Take her."

This time, I panic. I fight hard, yanking on my hands. I move my legs and a slap to my thighs makes me whimper. I still don't stop. I have to get these men away from me. My fighting does nothing aside from wear me out. Ayres grabs my throat.

"Stop fucking moving. We love the struggle. But you are messing with yourself. We are only going to go harder to make you wiggle more. Slaps are going to hurt worse. We are not stopping. It's best if you do."

I begin choking and the man grabs my throat even tighter. My mouth opens wide as his grip tightens. He holds my chin as he thrusts in and out of my mouth, taking my ability to bite down, away. He makes me choke then pulls back. At first I think he's finished but I quickly realize I was wrong. He shoves right back in.

"Yeah, keep it just like that. Don't move, let me have that tight little throat of yours, Kitten."

Ten

AYRES

I MOAN as I go balls deep into the girl's mouth. Kronos strokes his cock. Hypnos has wrestled her legs to a point where he's in between her legs now. He shoves straight into her. I can feel her blood curdling scream as he claims her. He pulls back, showing us her virginity. We all look at his cock in awe. She really was pure. My mind goes absolutely crazy.

I nut without delay and her body goes lax. She's in shock, it seems. I pull my cock out of her mouth and shut the door. Kronos is still kneeling in his seat as I take off. Hypnos looks at her, her eyes closed, tears running down her face. She's quiet—too quiet. But Hypnos still pushes into her fast and hard.

I drive home as the party in the backseat continues. The idea of getting to sample more of the kitten's body makes me speed.

"Tight and fucking perfect," Hypnos moans, jostling her body as he drives into her. "Going to make a perfect little sex toy."

Hypnos's words make me shift. I'm hard as a rock. Kronos

aims his dick at the girl and spews his seed. It paints along her chest and as I look in the mirror at her, my dick twitches and my heart begins to beat fast. *What the fuck?*

Damn, my dick is throbbing, ready to go again. I slap Kronos' ass and he turns to me. "Kiss him," Hypnos grunts. I look at Kronos and he smirks before kissing me, making me take my eyes off the road. We hit a bump and I pull away from Kronos.

"Fuck, let's get home before we die with how damn horny we are." Kronos buckles his seatbelt just as Hypnos comes into the girl's still bleeding pussy. I can't wait to lick it and drive her wild with orgasms. Make her beg me to stop.

Hypnos holds the girl as he pulls her to him. He's gentle. Something I didn't think he knew how to be. He has her head in his lap, stroking her hair. "You did good, Little Warrior. No more fighting now," he whispers.

My mind goes haywire. I've never seen him like this. He's talked more tonight than he has in years. The curls on the girl's head cover her face, but I can see the tears still flowing. She's calmed down for the moment. Her fight is gone. In a way, I hope it isn't gone forever. I like my little kitten with claws.

I pull into the driveway and Hypnos is humming to her, still stroking her hair. Kronos is quiet. Dammit, I can tell he's warring with himself. I've only seen him like this one time before.

"What are we going to do with her?" The concern in my voice surprises me. "She's a witness. We don't leave witnesses."

Hypnos yells out, "We keep her. We don't fucking kill her." We turn to him.

Kronos looks down at the girl. So, do I. It's like looking at a broken angel who lost her wings. "Do what now?"

"Yes, Hypnos is right, Ayres." I nod. You don't fight with Kronos. "We keep her as our pet. For now."

Eleven

HAYDES

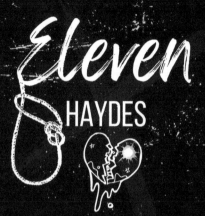

Ring.

Ring.

On the third ring, I answer my phone. Eyes closed, I don't think to look at the time. It's well past the time for me to be awake. I grumble anyway. "This better be good."

The hesitation on the other end hackles me. I sit up straight in my bed and look at the clock. Two in the morning. Who the fuck is calling me?

"I said, this better be good. Announce yourself and tell me what the fuck you want."

"Officer Torrez and I'm calling to inform you of a situation we have down here in Timberland."

Well, that got my attention quickly. I turn on the table lamp next to my bed and wipe the sleep out of my eyes. "Talk to me. Tell me what happened." The feeling that Charlotte is in danger awakens me faster than anything else in this world could. I almost have a small panic attack thinking of what could happen. She was safe eight hours ago. She should be home.

"The apartment building and the gas station in her neighborhood have both been blown up." Suddenly, my world tilts and I have to sit back down. I had just started pacing but stopped dead in my tracks at his words. Coldness seeps inside of me. My sweet little bird. Gone? *No.* I can't fathom it. It just can't be. Can it?

"Sir?" I know I need to answer, but the news has me dumbstruck. This should not have happened.

"Is she...? Is she dead?"

Officer Torrez him-haws about. "Well..."

My anger rises fast. My blood pressure has my ears ringing and I grit my teeth and demand, "Now, Torrez."

"Both buildings were leveled. The firefighters have not finished the initial look over, but there are no survivors thus far."

I hang up and throw my phone across the room—leading to it cracking into four pieces. I don't give a damn. My little bird. *No.* I argue with myself. She is not gone, can't be gone. Closing my eyes, I count to twenty. I race to my computer and pull up Charlotte's tracking device. Yes, all right, I'm a crazy motherfucker who must know where she is at all times. I went to bed last thinking she was fine. She was going to her friend's tattoo parlor and then she was going straight home. I even checked. She was at the tattoo parlor when I fell asleep. The guilt of it all makes me sick to my stomach.

At first the program refuses to work. I almost chuck my computer...but there it is. The little *beep, beep, beep.* She's alive. Or at least her necklace is. She never took it off. I will never forget the way she looked at me when I gave it to her on her fourteenth birthday.

Pulling up the map, I notice two things at once. One, she's at the Power's Estate. And two, there are four heat signatures in their house. Not three. She's alive. Oh, my little bird, thank god.

"I'm going to get you, you sadistic bastards," I whisper into the room. I don't know why I expect someone to talk back to me. It's not like there's anyone here to do so. My plan to take down the slimy bastards never included taking them out—but now? Now it does. They will pay. And then...they'll die.

Getting up, I make a beeline for Charlotte's old room. Opening the door, I can still smell her scent. She always smells like peonies and honeysuckle. There are pictures of my sweet little bird every year and stage of her life. Charlotte has grown into a strong woman. So beautiful. Sexy. She has absolutely no idea just how enticing she is.

I shouldn't have let her have her space. It was a damn mistake. One that I may be eating now that she may die, being in the hands of those bastards. If she dies, this entire city will burn. Burn to the ground, and then, I'll bury the ashes in a shallow grave and set them on fire. There will be nothing left.

"I'll get you back, sweet Charlotte," I mutter as I lay down on the bed that has a pile of her used panties on it. I roll around, soaking up her scent.

Twelve

CHARLOTTE

My body is far too tired to fight hard. I can't keep my legs up. I tremble as we enter a sparse area decorated in shades of gray and black. The coldness hits me, making me wince. They move me to a hall in the east of the house. No lighting except from one of the guy's phones.

"I just want to go home. Please," I beg. My stomach churns, I've been reduced to begging. They ignore me and drag me into a room that has me shivering. I know what this is. A BDSM torture room. My head is on a swivel, trying to take everything in all at once. Turning left, I see cages. Four in total. One for standing a person erect, one for making them squat in a cage meant for a small animal. I gulp and look away, not wanting to see the others.

Moving toward the back wall, my breath picks up pace as my eyes roam over everything. I didn't know what some of this stuff was. However, I did know what the crops, whips and chains were. *Why would anyone need all of this?* And why is there an X in the middle of the wall? Panic seeps through me.

"No," I yank against Ayres and try to stomp. All the jolting movement does is wear me out even more.

"Such a feisty kitten," Ayres laughs and takes me to a bench on the left side of the room. He places me on the bench, face down. The other two men waste no time in tying my legs so they are in a spread position. Ayres holds me down as I scream at them. Their only defense is laughter.

A hand comes down on my mouth at the same time a tongue licks down the length of my face.

"You have absolutely no chance of escape. This is your home until we kill you. Now shut up. Or, we can cut that tongue out of your mouth."

My entire body goes stiff as Ayres chuckles again. "Think she gets it now?" I hear the sound of zippers being undone and I wonder what more they could possibly do to me. Someone touches my butt before spreading my cheeks wide, humiliating me.

"No," I say, but my plea is silenced as Kronos shoves his cock into my mouth and the person behind me pushes into my very sore pussy. Screaming does nothing...except make Kronos fuck me harder. The feeling of the cold wood on the bench irritates my nipples. The emotions and feelings overwhelm me to the point that I'm wishing to just escape this body. He tugs at my nipples as he pounds me hard. It's painful. Painful enough that I'm trying to block it out. Tears run down my face as I choke on the cock in my mouth.

A stinging pain makes me flinch. The pain in my back causes me to wail around the cock in my mouth. The pain comes again, and I try to wiggle. *Fight!* I tell my brain. My body is under their control, though. Not mine.

"God damn, look at how her skin flushes with each slap of the whip," one of the men says and I flinch.

The whip comes back down and then it just seems to stop. I

feel the rope on my right leg loosen and my body rearranged by them until my knees are on the bench. The weight of the man on top of me is heavy, weighing me down. I try not to think about what they're doing.

I try to keep my mind blank—but it doesn't work. My body feels stimulated, and I hate it. My heart is breaking, and my mind shuts down right as the other man punches into my ass. The moan from the men makes me sick. They take every inch of my body hard, enjoying my struggle.

"Look at this sexy, wild, little virgin taking us like a well-paid slut." I'm not sure why, but the man's words make me angry. I buck and wiggle to no avail, so instead, I bite the man on his cock. Hard.

His scream is music to my ears. He had slipped his hands in my hair, forgetting my mouth was open because I allowed it. I kept my mouth clamped down, wanting to cause him even a fraction of the pain they've caused me.

"Fuck," he screams. He begins to slap my face. "Let go," he demands as he tries to release my mouth from his hard cock.

"Feisty, Little Warrior," the man behind me growls. He slips out of my ass and plunges back in. It's enough to make my mouth pop open in pain. The man in my mouth pulls his cock out and comes all over my face.

"Little bitch. You enjoy making me bleed?"

Slap.

Slap.

Slap.

Tears roll down my hot, battered cheeks. He picks up an item I've never seen before. It has a large red ball and straps. He wastes no time before shoving the ball into my mouth. The thing stretches my mouth beyond any limits I've ever felt before.

"She's taking all of me in that tight ass," the man grunts. I hate the way they're talking about me. And the feeling inside of me feels odd. Unexplainable. Before I can contemplate why the feeling is happening, both men come inside of me. They grunt and hold their cocks inside me while they spasm. I take every drop of cum deep inside of me.

They pull out and turn me on my back. "Damn, she looks pregnant," Kronos chuckles. I allow my eyes to roam over the men. Their cocks are wet, dripping from their tips and onto the floor. They look angry in a way. Then again, it's my first time to ever see a cock in real life.

"I just came and I'm ready to go again." I look at the one stroking his cock.

"God that ass felt great. Hell, now all I need is that sexy, feisty mouth."

Kronos plugs in his phone and puts the video of them taking my virginity up on a screen I hadn't seen before. "We keep her. She will be our pet. And cum dump. Pregnant."

He stops talking and I look at him. He just smirks. "That's right little rabbit, this is your life now. Our little whore." He seems to cum at that thought and another spray of wetness hits my body.

"Heirs. She will give us heirs," one says as another splash hits my face. The other two agree. They walk away from me, and I hear the locks engage. They've left me tied by my arms to the bench. I'm not moving anywhere.

Thirteen

HAYDES

Two weeks. I've been watching the Power's Estate the entire time they've had her. There is no sign of them leaving the house. They have their claws in *my* Charlotte. My basement, where I laid out all my plans to take the stepbrothers out, now has their names carved into the walls. But that's not all. No. I stole one of their whores from one of the whorehouses they have.

Am I ashamed that I've had the woman for four days and I've carved my name into her? No. No I'm not. I carved my name along her ass. Then I took a soddening iron and burnt the whore's breasts with my name in them. They'll know exactly who took their fucking whore. And they'll know exactly what I'll do to them—once I get a hold of the rat bastards.

I killed the woman after day three. Her whimpering pathetic pleas were getting on my damn nerves. I do, however, have a key to their whorehouse on Lamar Street. And every code to their offices. I know I'd picked the right girl to torture. Ah, the plan was simple. Place the bomb in the basement. After a certain amount of time, blow the son of a bitch up.

After I drop the girl in a box marked for delivery to the Powers boys' home, I smile and drive to the whorehouse. The rotten flesh will be horrendous to smell. Maggots will be crawling all over the girl by the time they get her. I chuckle, thinking how lovely it will be to see their faces. I have it on good authority that Ayres, in particular, liked this woman.

"Too bad boys." I drive in silence as I go over my plan to demolish their empire...one building at a time. The house shares a block with buildings that the Power's own, so when this thing explodes, it'll have a major effect.

Getting into the building is quite simple. *Too* simple. I show them the card that allows me entry and then I get the girl I want. I grin as she takes me to her room. I have to admit, they do have premium pussy at this establishment. There are no insignificant whores here. Each one looks better than the previous girl. Shame they'll all die tonight.

The woman I chose is undressing when I shoot her in the head. Her mouth is open in shock as she crumples to the floor. Good thing about this place, each room is soundproof. Stupid to have that when anyone could come in and tear the place down. Or maybe it's just arrogance. Doesn't matter. I make my way down to the basement of the house and plant my bomb.

Leaving through the back door, I walk the four blocks to my vehicle. I look at my tablet and notice that tonight, all the rooms are full, plus there's women on the floor, giving lap dances. It's a busy Friday night, maximum exposure. I set the time on my cell phone as I drive off.

Once I'm a safe distance away, I call the number on the cellphone attached to the bomb. *Boom.* The building crumbles at the touch of my finger. Even this far away, the earth shakes underneath me. And yet, all I can do is laugh. The way I see it, the less operations these motherfuckers have, the better. I call the explosion in and that's all I plan on doing.

Driving back home, I have to think that my sweet bird is still alive. That they haven't hurt her beyond repair. My hands hold the steering wheel tighter. If one piece of hair is out of place, I'll burn their entire worlds down. They'll have nothing left. I'll see to it. The feeling of vengeance covered in hate drives me to put my next action into place. I have to get my girl back. Because if I don't, no one is safe.

Fourteen

HYPNOS

WE'VE HAD the girl in the torture room for two weeks. She has refused to talk. Her only time to say anything is when she wants to use the restroom. Kronos and Ayres have not been down here since day nine. But I keep coming down, nonetheless. I know I can get the girl to talk. Today I've brought down hot water, soap, and strawberries. I'll figure out the way to get her to open up, one way or another.

Today she is in the corner, tied to the wall. Just where I left her yesterday. Her body is shaking, her little sleepy whimpers tell me she is dreaming. I don't feel remorse for taking her. And I don't feel guilty for the things we've done to her.

"Calm down," I bellow, and her eyes open, settling on me. She stops trying to move and stares at me, hatred in her eyes. Oh God, she's so beautiful. That hate and fear mingles together to form something otherworldly.

"I've brought you a warm bath. If you are a good girl, I will let you wash yourself." I take out the gag and she snarls. Her demeanor is so damn feral. So hot. My cock is already rock hard.

"Go to hell," she whispers. I laugh.

"Okay, so you aren't going to go down the easy road," I shake my head and shove the gag back into her mouth. Getting on my knees, I dip the cloth into the water.

"Kronos said if you were nice, you could be moved to a bedroom."

This gets her attention. She looks up at me as I move the cloth along her neck. We don't even know her real name and still, I feel for her. Not enough to let her go. No, just the opposite. I always want her in sight.

Taking my time, I move down her body. She moans. She's trying to hide it but I heard it. It was subtle, but I know what I heard. Even with the gag. Her nipples are hard from the cold. I smirk and rub the cloth along them. She closes her eyes. Even if she doesn't like this, or want it, her body can't lie about it.

"You little sex pot," I laugh again and touch her clit. She gasps, flinching. She's deliciously wet. "Let me help you with this." I rub each nipple before kissing down her neck. She whimpers again. Her body wants this.

She tries to close her legs. Too bad they remain chained to the wall. Fortunate for me. I move my fingers to her hole and shove two inside her. "Fuck, you are so tight, no matter how many times we use you."

Tears run down her face and she closes those beautiful eyes of hers. She's so damn vulnerable. I move my fingers slow and with purpose. Her back arches, those dirty hands are straining. Her lithe body shakes, telling me she's close to an orgasm. I can't wait to see her explode.

I admire her pebbled nipples, hard and ready for the taking. I suck each one, nibbling on them. I could spend hours playing with her, but instead, I pull back, making her struggle. It's a magnificent sight.

"Oh, Little Warrior. Stop fighting this," I move my hand along her wet lips. Pushing in and out, teasing her. She's moving away, but eager to come back. She loses herself for a moment, her eyes closed as I touch her deep within her silken flesh.

I take off the gag just to hear that sweet voice of hers. "Please." There's nothing more from her. Just *please*. I bet she's conflicted about why she's begging.

"Please what?" I taunt her. Those lips snarl at me. I wink at her as I push another finger into her wet pussy. "More, sweet Warrior?"

I watch as her body strains. Those hips move to the rhythm of my fingers. "I... I don't know what..." Dear Lord, has she never had an orgasm? Her face shows confusion and pleasure, twisted together. The fear is there, but her need is prevalent.

"Looks like the kitten is enjoying it," I turn to see Ayres here, leaning against the door. "Progress, thank goodness. Maybe Kronos will stop pouting."

"Hand me my knife, Ayres."

He walks toward me and picks up my Smith and Wesson stainless steel throwing knife, twirling it around his fingers.

"Kronos said to bathe her. Not give her pleasure." He hands me the knife and I snort.

"She is into it," I move the knife around her neck, nicking her along the collarbone. She gasps, shrinking away from me. The small amount of blood flowing down her naked body makes me smile and I lick the trail of red liquid.

"Sweet like honey," I bring my lips to hers, kissing her softly at first. Her tongue comes out to meet mine as I shove yet another finger into her. She screams, loud. That clenching pussy holds onto my fingers in a death grip.

Pulling back, I smile. Her orgasm juice is all over my fingers. Ayres unzips his pants. "Move Hypnos." I don't. Instead, I reach out with my tongue, licking the tip of his cock. The strangled sound coming from him is so unlike him.

"Watch him, Little Kitten. He is going to show you how this is done without teeth while you tell me your name." I look over at our girl. She looks dazed, but she is willing to watch. That is until Kronos walks in. She shrinks all the way back into the corner. Her eyes travel down, embarrassment and terror filling her entire body.

"We don't have time for fucking around. Get her cleaned up. We have to get going." Kronos turns around and leaves. Not before I see the jealousy in his eyes. Ayres zips himself back up, cursing and mumbling about *fucking work*. I go back to cleaning the girl up. I'm drying her off when she whispers.

"Charlotte."

Fifteen

CHARLOTTE

THEY'VE LEFT me alone for a long time and I've had a lot of time to sit with my conflicting thoughts. I'm a mix between scared and turned on. The men haven't hurt me since the last time they were all in the room with me. Only the guy with the knife fetish comes in regularly. I've done good staying quiet. It keeps me away from their torture. Today he came in and was gentle. No more demanding talk. Not today. He played with me, though, touching my body and making me have the most amazing explosion from my center. I didn't know I could do that. Or that I wanted it. I'm just worried they'll do this to me again.

And another question I've been pondering...why was looking at Hypnos taking Ayres' cock in his mouth so...hot? I tremble as chilly air hits my body. This is the worst part. They turned on the air, making me freeze.

"Hello?" I call out in hopes they'll get me out of here. I seem to call out for hours. But they never come. Not until I feel sleep trying to take me.

"Would you shut up?" My head pops up, startled. Kronos stands before me.

"Would you release me?"

He slaps me, forcing my head to the left.

"You've got a smart mouth," he snarls at me. My heart feels like it's about to beat out of my chest. I can't believe I'm provoking this man. It does get him to react, though. He unhooks my arms and then my legs.

"Thank—"

Slap.

I cry out, not expecting that next slap. He grasps my hair and yanks me up to him.

"So, fucking bold. It's like you purposefully try to piss me off."

I look at him, not saying anything because I'm afraid he will tie me up again. Instead, I just stare. He shakes his head, keeping a firm grip on my hair, dragging me from the room.

"My step-brothers believe you are good enough to have a bedroom. I agree, but with one slight hitch. You are going to prove to me that you deserve such generosity."

Before I can say anything, he throws me in a room. This room has a king size bed in the middle. Nothing more. An ensuite bathroom to the left, but I don't have time to think about any of the things in this room. Kronos yanks me to the bed and forces me on my knees.

"You want to stay in here?"

Those mean eyes pierce through me as I slip down to my knees. My legs hurt. I haven't used them in so long that the walk to the bedroom wore me out. I know this is a step in the direction of getting out of here. I just have to play along. Or at least...I hope it's a step in the right direction. With these men, you never know. "Yes, I would like that."

Kronos smiles, "Then you have a choice to make. You can willingly play with my cock and I will let you stay in this room. Or you can do this the hard way and I will put you in the animal cages."

Gulping, I look at his hands as he unzips his pants. "H... how do I play with you?" My voice is nothing more than a whisper. He begins to chuckle at me, mocking me.

"Such an innocent thing. Even after everything you've had done to you, you still know nothing." He brings my hand to his cock and wraps it around his thickness.

"Now move it slowly up and down." He pushes his free hand into my hair and forces me to look up at him. "Little Rabbit, squeeze it a little harder."

Looking at him while stroking him off is embarrassing. I blink and try not to look away, but I can't keep eye contact. I look down and gasp as he squeezes my hair in his hand. "Eyes on me."

The door opens and I feel tempted to look back at the person coming in. I don't though. I keep my eyes locked on Kronos. I stroke him a bit harder and a little faster.

"What, Ayres?"

"We got a problem down at Kelley's Lounge."

Kronos goes rigid. "All right. Tell me what happened." The silence is deafening as I look at Kronos. He turns cold even as his cock throbs in my hands.

"Kelley's Lounge has been bombed."

I don't know what a *Kelley's Lounge* is, but it shocks me nonetheless. I take a deep breath as I let his cock go. There's no way that he'd stay hard. Right?

"Did I tell you to stop stroking me?" He demands my attention once more, pulling my head in a rough fashion. My neck arches in a precarious angle.

"No."

"No, what?" I look at him confused. No, what? What did he expect me to say?

"What do..." He slams my mouth down on his cock. My mouth opens wide to take his girth and I choke as he pushes me all the way down on him.

"No, Sir," he says as he forces me down past my gag reflex. "It's a respect thing. You are aware of common courtesy for your superiors. Aren't you?"

His words make me angry. How dare he? He is a killer and a rapist. He can't believe I'll just bow to him. Before I can process, he yanks me back up.

"Well?"

I have a choice to make right here. I could fight. But I don't want to test the cages out. I could also keep my little bit of freedom. I could escape easier out here in this spacious room.

"I'm sorry, Sir. I meant no disrespect." His glare at me withers. I tremble as he grips my hair once again, forcing me back down.

Sixteen

KRONOS

I was being an ass. I knew this. But I wanted to hear that sugar sweet voice call me Sir. As she did, my cock seeped pre-cum. I'm fucking turned on and I know the hornier I get, the more of an ass I'm going to be.

"Get the car ready to leave in five minutes," I tell Ayres as I take control of her head and fuck her mouth. Her gags are music to my ears. I laugh as I come down her throat.

"Even if you have a smart mouth, it is good for a cum dump." I hold her head down as the last drop of cum slides down her throat. I pull her from my mouth. "Now, you will stay in this room and when I get back, you'll do everything I say. Do you understand me?"

I watch her look up at me, slobber and cum running down her chin. "Yes Sir." I stroke her face. Such a soft face. No scars or rough patches. Nothing like the whores I used to bang.

"Good girl."

"Thank you, Sir." I let her face go and leave the room.

Fucking feelings are creeping up on me. I can't think about, much less explain, how she's making me feel. Hypnos meets me in the hallway with his tablet. Looking at the report, I feel extreme anger take place over anything I was just feeling for my little Charlotte.

"Thirty-two dead. Seventeen in intensive care. The explosion took not only Kelley's Lounge, but the brewery beside it. And the skate shop behind." I listen to what Hypnos has to say. This is a shit storm. "I've already called the hospital. We will cover the bills. I've sent messengers ahead to all of the families."

I nod as we make our way to the car. "Do not leave this house Ayres." Ayres looks at me and I smirk. Ayres hates sitting on the sideline, but I can't leave Charlotte with Hypnos. Hypnos is too sentimental toward the girl. Hell, I don't trust myself alone with her; there is no telling what I might do to her.

When we get to the whorehouse, I become even more enraged. This attack was personal. No one blows up an entire city block in the dingiest part of town without it being personal. "The drug value we lost is estimated around two hundred and fifty thousand. The night deposit is estimated around seventy-five thousand."

Fuck. My mind splits into different thoughts. *Who the fuck did this?* I get out of the car and head straight toward the back of the building, or at least where the back used to be. Looking over the area, I move some rubble around until I find what I'm looking for. The small lock box is open. Only my stepbrothers and I know about this box.

"This was a personal mission," I growl at Hypnos.

"Yep. And that's not all." I turn to him. There's a message on his tablet. Looking at the words, my blood boils in my veins.

"Officer Torrez, lead investigator, rules this as accidental due to a small gas leak."

Fucking Officer Torrez has been after us for a decade. Of

course she ruled it as a bogus gas leak. I groan and throw the little safe box down. The plans to expand our empire, gone. Blown up and stolen.

"We have to pull all the cameras to find out who was here. We must find who's trying to encroach on our territory."

Hypnos is quiet once again, pecking away at the damn tablet. "I'll get them. For now, we have to get to the docks. The men are having problems with the machines. They keep saying it's some kind of override that's stopping them from working."

I slam the car door. "For fuck's sake. What the bloody hell is going on? Who the hell grew some balls all of a sudden?"

Hypnos drives us to the docks in silence. I stare out the front window, contemplating whether our little rabbit has something to do with this trouble. And why I feel like she's going to be the doom of us all. *And I wonder why I don't mind that at all?*

Hypnos fishes out a spot for us at the docks and I look at the chaos going down. Before I get out of the car, Hypnos grabs my arm and I instinctively turn to him. "What?"

"Charlotte Camillo."

His words hit me like a ton of bricks. "The fuck?" *Camillo.* That name changed my life ten years ago and I never thought I'd hear it again. Cold chills run down the length of my spine. My hands shake with a feeling I never thought I'd have again.

"Her fingerprints finally came back. She's the young girl *you* let live." Hypnos' voice sounds like it's in a tunnel. I don't think I could move if I wanted to. My mind explodes as he keeps talking, his words sound far away as my mind spins. Talk about a full circle. As I get out of the car, I walk to the docks and it hits me.

"Haydes." That motherfucker. We were partners before Ayres caught him trying to steal our territory.

"Exactly what I was thinking. Besides, doing a little bit of research shows he went legit. He's a retired social worker. And guess who one of his kids was?"

I didn't need to guess. "Charlotte."

"Bingo."

Seventeen
HAYDES

I WATCH them scramble to put the pieces together. A smile creeps up on my face—enjoying that they have no clue what to do from here. One minute they were at the whorehouse, the next they were getting a call about their docks. It's a bait and hook type of situation. One that I know how to do well. It's how I kept Charlotte in my care all those years.

Knowing my enemy, I knew they would go to investigate the explosion. I also knew that Kronos would want to get home as soon as possible because he was uncertain about Charlotte. I've watched them with her. Hypnos is in love with her. He's a prick and what he does to her is bullshit. But he loves her. Ayres isn't far behind. I know this and that means it'll only take Kronos falling for her for them to keep her forever. That's not an option.

So, I made a diversion. I can't let them catch on to my plan. Not yet anyway. With the click of an app on my tablet, I hacked the secure system on the docks. Every machine turned on. Every man working there scrambled to turn off the machines. They didn't know they couldn't. I'm controlling them from Hypnos' computer, and I laugh at that thought. The arrogant bastards just don't think anyone *would* or *could* hack them. Too late.

This will set back their operations as I move the machines to knock product into the water. One machine even overheated. I chuckle at the idea of a fire going off in their drug stash. Ah the irony, they tried to bring the drugs into their legitimate business and it's all going up in flames, literally.

Hypnos will be onto the situation in a matter of minutes, so I put in a black box code that will keep him from his computers at the office. He'll know someone hacked his system. It will make him a formidable foe once he catches wind of the issue. Too bad I'm leaving a trace that will show him it was one of his own employees that back stabbed them.

The moan catches my attention and I turn to my other tablet. "Little bird," I whisper as I watch as she struggles to get out of the room. I growl at myself for being turned on. She bangs her fist on the door, kicking it. Such a temper. Her temper—in the past—made me rock hard. Now I'm seeping cum, wanting more from her.

"Hold on Charlotte, I'm coming for you. I swear little bird, I'll get you out of there. Just stay focused sweet girl." I know she can't hear me. But I need those words out in the universe. I need to keep hope alive. Just seeing her naked should enrage me. That body is supposed to be mine. I'm rock hard, ready to fuck her, wanting to claim her as mine.

Frustrated, a growl comes from deep within my throat. I turn the tablet's noise off and put it in my passenger seat. I have business to address. I pick up my cell and call the security company. Just as I planned, my contact comes through for me.

Within seconds, I have access to every security system in the house. I also have access to all the locks on the doors. I smile. Now I just have to be patient for the right time to help my little bird.

Eighteen

CHARLOTTE

As soon as they leave me, I try to escape the room. "Duh, who wouldn't try it?" I'm talking to myself again. It's locked from the outside. I sigh. I should have known. Biting my lip, I go to the bathroom. I haven't had a real shower in almost two weeks. Or maybe it has been two weeks. Time is hard to figure out when I don't know what time it is or what day it is. Even though Hypnos washes me every day, it isn't the same.

I explore the bathroom first, searching for any hidden-in-plain-sight weapons. None. Of course there isn't. I do, however, find my favorite shampoo and soap. A razor and a blow dryer. I nibble on my lip, contemplating what I could do with a plastic razor.

I gasp as my train of thought turns dark. No. Suicide is not an option. I find a fluffy towel and even a gown. No panties. No bra. Well, beggars can't be choosers. I take a long, hot shower, enjoying the warmth. I bend over to take a moment to shave my legs as a sound in the room makes me jump.

"Well, well, well."

I look up and find Ayres standing against the door frame. "You made yourself right at home, didn't you?"

I cower as he stares at my body. The lust in his demeanor is recognizable. I watch as his eyes flame as they roam over my body, taking me in, inch by inch.

"I..."

"Oh stop. You're allowed a bath. Now get out of there before Kronos and Hypnos find you in here pampering yourself. They may think I'm spoiling you."

He reaches for me, but I step back. His eyes flare with anger. Ayres steps into the tub, dominating the space. "You think you can move away from me?"

His hand comes out, grabbing my throat and pushing me against the wall of the shower.

"No, I'm... I'm sorry." The plea in my voice makes me sound weak but I don't care. I don't mean to upset him. I fear him. What do they expect? My submission? Or maybe my gratitude?

His laugh holds no humor. "Not as sorry as you will be after I'm finished with your punishment." He squeezes my throat hard and my lungs seize.

"Ay... Ayres..." I choke out. He stares at me with those steel eyes and I shrink against the wall.

"You don't get to say my name." He pulls me out of the shower and pushes me to the ground. He forces my head into a ring on the floor. It locks and as I move—well, try to move—I go nowhere. I'm stuck. Ayres positions me so that I'm on my knees. He grabs my arms and brings them behind me. This ends my struggle. He opens the sink cabinet and pulls out chains with cuffs on them. The cold metal grazes my skin, making me shiver.

"It's time you learned your place." His menacing words send a chill down my spine. I don't understand any of this. I mean, maybe I should have asked for the shower. I begin to cry as he puts the cuffs on my ankles. Then I hear it and my heart all but stops beating. He's undoing his zipper. Dread fills me. I'm not ready for more of his punishments. He's going to rape me again. I feel it. It doesn't matter though. He's going to do whatever he wants no matter what I say. No matter how much I beg. He doesn't answer me right away and panic courses through me. *What is he doing?*

"I bet that sweet little pussy is wet for me, isn't it?" he says from behind me. His fingers touch my ass and I wince. It's still sore from sitting on the cold concrete in the torture room. He wastes no time before sticking his dick inside of my butt—with no lube. I scream.

"Stop. Stop please." My feet kick, my arms straining as I try, but fail, to get away from him. He slaps my ass on each cheek five times and I can't control my body jerking in reaction.

"Shut up or I'll shut you up." An agonizing jolt goes through me as he tightens something onto my labia. It feels like a thousand needles prickling me at once.

"Ah, look at that clamp. So sexy," he grits out before shoving a cold, round item into my body. My eyes close on their own as my mind works out what he's doing to me. He adds another ball, and they begin to move. My face contorts as they start vibrating, catching me off guard.

"If they fall out of your pussy, I'm going to tan that ass. Keep them in, Kitten."

I don't know how. They keep pulsating and with each vibration they slip a bit further. He shoves two fingers inside of me and pushes the balls around as a lick of pain and pleasure runs through me. My confusion spikes. I shouldn't enjoy any of this...but the pleasure plays with my mind, making me forget about what's actually going on here.

"There we go, Little Kitten. Let's see how much we can

make you moan for Daddy." I blink in awe at his words. Did he just call himself Daddy? And... and did I like it? My body trembles. My entire world shifts with need and want, but pain brings me back all too soon.

Ayres shoves his cock into my ass in one long, swift push. I cry out, begging him to stop but he doesn't. No. He holds my ass still, not that I'm going anywhere, fucking me harder and faster. "That's it, take Daddy's cock."

Nineteen

AYRES

That pussy is tight. *Delicious.* I ram my cock deep inside her once I pull my fingers from her. Even as she whines. As she pleads for me to stop. There is no stopping. Not when I'm ten inches deep, spanking that ass with her little pussy clenching me.

Her moans turn from whimpers of protest to *please don't stop.* That name calling got her going. "Oh, Kitten. You like when I call myself Daddy, don't you?"

"Yes." That whisper must have cost her because her body deflates after she utters it. I run a hand along her spine, tingling her nerves with my strokes. She shivers and I smirk.

"Louder."

"Yes." The word comes out in a moan. It comes out broken and I know she's trying to fight what she's feeling. Mind and body at war with one another.

"Say it right." I jerk her hips back into me. Hard. Rougher than before. I need to show her just how serious I am. Need to show her I'm in charge, and she doesn't get a say in how she obeys me.

I hit that special spot in her as I reach around her and flick her engorged clit. She screams and tries to back into me and I chuckle as I push into her, holding her still.

"Now, little girl."

"Yes." She howls out as her body gives way to an orgasm. "Daddy," she yells, then mumbles it in a chant. It is as if she is praying to me. To not stop. To keep pounding into that pliant, wet pussy of hers.

"Good girl," I growl and slap her ass hard enough to leave a handprint. "You didn't ask for permission to cum, little one."

Her whimpering turns into a growl. Her body begins to go rigid again. I know she's coming out of her high from her orgasm. I pull those perfect, hard nipples and squeeze them until she begs me to stop. Her begs are beautiful. Soulful.

I don't stop. No, her begging only makes me force my cock deeper into her so I can play with those balls that are straining to get back together. They're vibrating along my firm cock and her body is pulsating. I pull out and Charlotte screams. I know that the balls just crashed into each other. They sent pleasure through her body, shaking her. They'll continue to vibrate until I turn them off. *If* I turn them off. Her tiny body quivers, trying to fight the impeding orgasm from happening.

"Let it go, my sweet Kitten. Your body wants this. Just give in to Daddy."

My words make my cock jolt as I slam back into her, her body giving way to that magnificent orgasm still lingering within her. Her screams for *Daddy* are such a damn turn on. She's unable to resist my hard fucking now. Those vibrating balls pulsate against the both of us and she begins to chant at me again.

"Daddy..." her little body tries to move back against me once more.

"Daddy, please..." Her begging makes me push into her one last time. Stroking her clit a little harder. Faster. Her pants are chaotic. Her hips try to wiggle but her moans keep coming. Those begging words on repeat.

"Cum for me, my little pet." I feel my cock seize up and spurt my baby juice all over her pussy. She has a chain reaction and comes with me. Her body seizing up as she screams my name loud. For a good two minutes I stay in her, coating every inch of her body, making sure she knows that if we aren't careful, she's going to be pregnant. I can't think of anything I want more than that.

Pulling out of that warm body, I whisper in her ear, "Good pet. Now, you'll stay here until I return."

I stand up, putting my cock back into my pants and washing up. My cum drips from her body and I take a picture. For two reasons: to keep a picture of her on my phone and to send it to my stepbrothers. To show them I have her under control and that her pussy is primed for them to come take it.

I start to walk out of the bathroom and she whimpers for me to let her go. I ignore her and turn the balls on high. As I make it to her bedroom door, she's already screaming. I laugh, knowing she'll have a hell of a time with those balls because I'm not turning them off.

Once downstairs, I go to the kitchen to make myself something to eat. I wonder if my feisty kitten will allow me to feed her while she's on the ground. I grow hard just thinking about it. Fuck, I haven't been soft in almost two damn weeks. This is a good thing. But hell, my poor cock can only take so much. I laugh out loud as I start making a sandwich, wondering if the girl knows how to cook. Cause if she does, hell, I'll shackle her and confine her to the kitchen just to watch those perky tits bounce around.

Before I finish my food, my step brothers come through the doors. Hypnos looks pissed off. But then again, he always looks pissed. It's his go to emotion. It's Kronos that worries me, though. When he's dead silent, something is eating at him.

"What's up guys?" Hell, I thought the picture would have gotten them here sooner, ready to fuck like wild animals. Surely me sending them the picture didn't piss them off.

"We have to kill her," Kronos says and I pause, food halfway to my mouth.

"What the fuck Kronos?" I'm attached and don't want her dead, but what the ever-loving-fuck is this about?

Hypnos looks ready to punch Kronos. This is the reason he looks so pissed. He doesn't agree with Kronos.

"Charlotte Camillo." I throw my sandwich down, my stomach turning sour as I look up. That name, I know it. An odd, guilty feeling rushes through me. "No fucking way." *Fuck.* What a mess.

Kronos sighs as his hands clench, "Yes. I let her live ten years ago. We thought she had bled out. Instead, here she is, in our house, being our pet."

Hypnos looks at both of us. "It's better this way, better she's alive instead of dead. Now she owes *us* for being generous."

Kronos shakes his head. "You know we don't leave witnesses and I swore that night I should have killed her. I didn't and now here she is. The only witness to our crimes once again."

"Enough," I say with venom in my voice. I look at both my stepbrothers. "I never go against either of you. But this is not up for debate. She is ours. Hypnos is right. We are getting revenge not only on her for now, but the past as well. Let's just see how it plays out."

They both look at me. The easy-going brother who never says anything to defy them has just defied both of them. Hypnos just nods in agreement with me. Usually, that means Kronos will consider stepping down and reassessing his thoughts.

"Fine. We don't kill her. Not yet. But if she causes us any more trouble, you know what must be done."

Twenty

CHARLOTTE

Moans ring out from the room. I'm not sure who it is, because in my dream I am running and the wind hits me in my face, making me laugh as my hair gets into my eyes. As a tongue enters my body, I wake up with a jolt. I didn't know I had fallen asleep. The balls were going crazy and after the fourth or fifth orgasm, I couldn't hold onto consciousness any longer. My body quit on me. My mind quieted and off to dreamland I went.

I blink my eyes open to clear the sleep from them. It's a struggle without my hands. My vision blurs as I try to take in my surroundings. "Ah, she's awake." The deep bass booms over me. Kronos is here. I shiver as I look in front of me. My body goes rigid. Ayres sits in front of me with food in his hand and a sarcastic smile. A hand touches my backside and I shiver.

"Little Warrior," Hypnos calls to me as I take a deep breath, trying to clear my head. I don't want to feel the pleasure.

"Please, let me go." I know this was a useless question. A stupid question. But I have to try, right? They laugh at me.

"The fact you are alive right now is because you have good pussy. The minute you become boring, you're dead. Just like your mother."

The entire room goes silent. The static electricity in the room is palpable. I whimper as my breath hitches and I begin to bawl loud, gut-wrenching sobs.

"Feed her and get her in the bed. We got shit to do. No more fucking her until we get this cluster fuck cleared up."

The bathroom door slams shut and Ayres sighs. My soul is shattered. The fact he knew—no *they* knew—that my mother is dead and Kronos just threw it in my face...it rips me to shreds. I can't stop from feeling like I'm drowning from my own tears.

Thrust.

Thrust.

Thrust.

Hypnos is playing with me, trying to keep me from being inside of my head. His fingers thrust harshly into my body. Four fingers, deep inside me. I don't like it. It's painful. Very painful. I sob as Ayres unhooks my neck. He pulls my head up and strokes my face.

"Shh. Focus on Daddy, Kitten."

I feel my mind battling all the feelings. The rampage of mixed emotions. The idea that I enjoy Ayres calling himself Daddy doesn't escape me. But those four fingers in me are stretching my body too much. It's hurting me.

"Are you going to be a good girl?"

My tears stop me from speaking, so I nod. Hypnos pulls my body back against his. Ayres lets go of my face and Hypnos pulls me to his chest.

"There now, Little Warrior. Let's get you cleaned up. Then you eat. We'll let you sleep. You'd like that, yes?"

I tremble as he talks. My tears begin to recede. How do they know about my mom? And why won't they just let me go?

"Good little Kitten. Daddy and Hypnos are going to make it all better." My pussy clenches as Ayres—Daddy—talks. He makes me feel as if I'm in a warm cocoon. I don't know why. But for once, I just let it go. I'm too tired emotionally to fight.

They pull me off the floor and Hypnos turns on the water. Ayres leaves and for a split second, I wonder where he went. I shake my head. No. I can't let...let them get to me like this. I just can't. The idea of succumbing to them will be the end of me. The ruin of me. No. I have to fight. I sniffle as we get into the shower. He's fully clothed, but it doesn't faze him. He turns me toward him, tipping my head back into the water.

"Relax, I'm going to take care of you."

My eyes close as he begins to massage my hair with a thick shampoo. My heart rises into my throat. He's being kind, but I can't trust this moment. They'll hurt me again. Kronos for sure. His words freeze me with shock.

"I said relax."

I gasp as he yanks my hair. "Stay out of that head when I'm trying to be nice to you."

My lower lip quivers. "I... I'm sorry Hypnos."

His breath falters. "Say it again." His demand is full of pure lust.

"I'm sorry Hypnos." I know I have no choice but to do what he wants. To make sure he doesn't hurt me like Ayres and Kronos. His hands travel back into my hair, massaging me, then pushes me back into the water. He washes my hair and then turns me back to face the water. He hugs me deep into his body and bites my ear.

"Such a good little warrior. I'm proud of you. Just let me wash you. Let me soothe that throbbing body."

Twenty-One

HAYDES

THE DOWNSIDE of watching the house is that I can hear and see everything going on inside. It broke my heart when Charlotte started crying over her mother. The bastard Kronos is a callous prick. It's insane how much the hurt emanating from Charlotte killed me. I watch now as Ayres goes into the bedroom, pulls down the covers and leaves her food by the table. It's just a sandwich and an apple. I honestly thought they were going to make her starve. Fruits have been her main diet for the last few days. I had to pull out my stress ball to keep myself from barging into that house.

Kronos paces back and forth in his office, muttering to himself about karma and how life is a bitch. He's at an impasse, and I know it. Too bad he never took my advice all those years ago. I am quite sure he knows I'm behind this. And I'm all right with that. He needs to know I will stop at nothing until I burn them down. All of them. They took the one thing they should have never taken.

I digress. I flip back to the bathroom and watch Charlotte

struggle with her emotions. It's clear on her face that she's in a battle. Her body wants one thing. Her heart is breaking. It pains me to see the tears fill her eyes. Such a brave girl. Before I know what I'm doing, I'm stroking my cock as she steps out of the shower with Hypnos. He strips his clothes and uses a towel on himself first, then on Charlotte. She stands there, conflicted, and all I can do is look at her beauty.

"Boss."

I put my cock back into my pants as the door opens and my assistant comes sauntering in. "What?"

"Operation Lion is a go."

I nod at the woman that has been with me for fifteen years. She and I used to be lovers. That is, until *she* fell in love with Ayres. She betrayed the brothers for me. But still, I couldn't let that grudge go. I could feel the hate and loyalty warring within me.

"Excellent," I say, just as I pull out my gun and shoot Officer Torrez in the left eye. "That will be all." I chuckle as she drops to the floor. Dead. I've been waiting to do that for fifteen years. And now, I can continue my work.

I check that Operation Lion really is ready to go. The first four steps have been completed. I need to make sure that the last step is done. My fingers twitch to make it happen. To complete what I have been trying to carry out for ten years.

"Little bird, I'm coming."

Twenty-Two

CHARLOTTE

HYPNOS SITS me down on the bed. I shudder, unsure what to expect. I know it's going to be something bad, I can feel it. It's always something bad. Or at least it has been for the last two weeks. I look at him and he hands me a sandwich as I take a deep breath. "Are... are you going to hurt me now?"

I know it's stupid to ask. Every time I ask, it seems like I just irritate them more. He looks at me before grabbing my neck and forcing me to look him straight in his eyes. Shaking, my breath falters. I feel like time has stopped as he holds me eye to eye with him. "Do you want me to hurt you, Little Warrior?"

Shaking my head no, I feel the tears filling my eyes. "N... No," I plead with him and he releases me and starts laughing. "If I had more time, I'd whip you and force you to take it up the ass. But as it is, you are going to get a reprieve. I don't have time for you right now."

He walks out the door and I can breathe again. Finishing the sandwich, I look around the room. I go over to the windows and I look down, gulping. I'm in the woods. I can't even try to open the windows. The idea of falling into the unknown down below makes me queasy. I back away from the window and immediately feel a smidge better.

Getting a hold of myself, I take a deep, deep breath. Then I open the window and an alarm starts blaring. I shut the window quickly, but apparently not quickly enough, because all three men burst into my room. "I..." The words escape me. I should have known better. *Dammit.*

"I..."

"Were you trying to run, little rabbit?" Kronos stalks over to me, growling.

"No," I say softly, and he steps right into me, pushing me back into the wall.

"I believe you're lying." He's so close to me. "My brothers have been way too soft on you. I should have known better than to allow you to be in the guest room."

My brain catapults into overdrive. If he takes me back to the dungeon, I'll never get out of here. I do the only thing I can think of, and I kiss him. I kiss him with all my might and still don't know how to kiss worth a damn. I'm used to being forced to open my mouth so their tongues and dicks can gain entry. But here I am, running my hands along his chest and kissing him. Kissing him to make him hush. To rethink things.

His hands grab my hips and push me hard against the wall. So hard I know I'll be bruised. He deepens the kiss, pushing his tongue into my mouth before pulling back. "You truly were a virgin when we took you. You kiss like shit." He pulls back and I blush. Embarrassment heats my skin. First from my action, but also from his words. His words cut deep. Deeper than they should.

I don't retort. I know better. It would be useless, and I would just get into trouble anyways. Trouble I don't need right now.

"I'm sorry."

He looks at me and his nostrils flare. "What are you sorry for?" I don't understand what he doesn't comprehend here.

"For opening the window and... and not knowing how to kiss. I'm sorry."

I look for the other two but they're already gone. Kronos' hands touch my thighs softer, and he pulls me into him. "You truly are so innocent." He's in awe, it seems. His eyes turn a darker green—I could stare into them for days. I really do need to get out of here. My sanity depends on it.

His lips touch mine and then he backs away. "Do not try to open the windows or the doors. You do, it will send an alarm. You get one chance. Don't fuck it up."

"Yes Kronos, I understand." It feels like this is the only way I can get them to believe I'm going to be a good girl. It works for now. Kronos leaves me to my thoughts and my boredom. I search the room high and low for something to use as a weapon. Nothing.

After an hour or so, I give up. I sit on the bed with my thoughts of how mean Kronos is. How do they know my mother's dead? The only logical explanation comes to mind. They're connected to the accident. Those green eyes Kronos has are unforgettable. The men that have me hostage here are capable of treacherous acts. This includes killing my mother. Even if I have to *pretend* to be their fuck toy, I'm getting out of here. One way or another.

Twenty-Three

HYPNOS

Kronos comes down from Charlotte's room and the look on his face says it all. The girl got to him when she kissed him, penetrated his walls. It isn't necessarily a deep emotion, but one of wonderment. I figure it's going to take a huge act for Kronos to relinquish his feelings.

"She got to you, huh?" Ayres doesn't know how to leave well enough alone. He's all about poking the damn bear.

For once, Kronos doesn't engage with him. Instead, he looks at his phone and his eyes turn to stone. "This a joke, Hypnos?" He shoves his phone in my face and I nearly drop my spoon full of pudding.

"No. Who the fuck took this?"

Ayres comes ambling over and looks at the photo. "Someone has access to the cameras, then?"

I pick up my own phone and look at the anonymous email. Someone is playing against the ivy leagues and they should have known better. "I'll figure it out."

Kronos and Ayres leave the house after telling me I *better fucking figure it out.* Kronos is livid. There are pictures of every room in the house sent to our phones. And what's worse is that there are pictures of Kronos and I at Kelley's Lounge—and at the docks. Someone is tailing us and surveying us. This isn't something the police would do. Someone is playing games with us.

The lights start flickering as I make my way to the house. That's odd. Why are they flickering? It only usually happens in the middle of a category two thunderstorm. I power up the computer system and start going through every system we have. There's something wrong. There's no sign of a hack. And there is no sign of an outside person tampering with footage from the house or the lounge. The docks, we knew there was something fishy going on there, but still, it all points to an inside job. Which I know isn't the case. Our men know better. They're too stupid to know how to hack.

"Son of a bitch," I mutter as I look at the time. It's taken me an hour to back trace the logs on the dock. This is pissing me off. And every ten minutes a new picture keeps coming into the phone. I know the others are getting them too because we've been texting each other about them. The pictures show the dungeon room. That room is secure. *How?*

Distracted, I must say, I'm enjoying the picture show even if I am going to have to hunt down the stupid fuck that's doing this and kill him.

Kronos: *Make the pictures stop. I can't concentrate on killing rat bastards with a hard dick.*

Ayres: *Dude, seriously, these pictures of Charlotte sleeping are hot. But I need to be able to interrogate assholes without the constant dinging of my damn phone.*

I ignore their texts. I'm in the middle of running a trace when my computer screen goes on the fritz. Before I can do much more, a burning *H* appears on my screen. And then it's gone. My computer fades to black right in front of my eyes. The lights go out, too, and I hear water running. *What the fuck?* I get up and use my cellphone's flashlight to make my way to the door. It doesn't budge. *Locked?* Who the hell locked my door?

Charlotte screams and I turn cold. Fuck, I forgot about Charlotte. *Has someone found her? Fuck.* I have to get out of here. Before I can pry open the door, everything stops. Just like it's another day, like nothing had just happened. Dead silence. The water goes off and the electricity buzzes back to life. My computer screen sits on a blank screen.

Hypnos: *Someone has hacked our main frame. I'm going to start digging. Kill whoever you are killing right now and then go check our businesses. Do not call, the phone lines may not be secure. This is a problem network wide. I'm on the hunt.*

Kronos: *Everything stable at the house?*

Ayres: *Do we need to come back?*

Hypnos: *Everything is stable. I just checked, it was a power surge, but someone is playing games. I'm going to tear this fucker's world apart. Charlotte is safe in her room; the alarms are up and running. Just check on everything else.*

Kronos: *Done.*

Ayres: *You got it.*

Whoever is behind this is going to pay. No one fucks with us. I double down my efforts and more time passes by. I check on Charlotte in the monitor. She lays in a ball, holding a pillow to her chest. Her face is so peaceful, angelic. I want to believe that she wants to be here with us. But I know I'm daydreaming again for happiness. There is no happiness for the wicked.

Twenty-Four

CHARLOTTE

THE LIGHTS KEEP FLICKERING. I don't understand why and
when the water comes on, I scream. Everything goes eerily
silent. *Deadly* silent. Everything is becoming too much. I lay in
the bed, pulling the covers over my head. I don't want to face
what's going on. The door stays locked. The alarm system is on.
It's all too much. My brain shuts down and my eyes close as
sleep takes me.

"Charlotte."

"Wake up Charlotte."

Dreamland feels too good to wake up from. Shaking, I pop
open an eye and look around. Hypnos is hovering over me. I
shiver at the sight.

"Shh. I'm not going to hurt you. You were moaning and I
came in here to see if you were all right."

Laughter almost bubbles up. Am I all right? That's hilari-
ous. How can this man think I'm even remotely *all right*?

"How can I be all right Hypnos?" The words flutter away

from me as I stare at him. His eyes turn cold as ice as his big hand lurches at me, encircling my throat.

"Ungrateful," he snarls at me. My entire body goes rigid as he throws the covers off my body, forcing me to look at him. To be bare to him. My body trembles with fright as he moves, spreading my legs.

"Please, I'm sorry Hypnos." My words mean nothing to him but he releases my neck anyways. "Too late." He pulls his cock out of his pants and shoves himself deep inside me. I scream as he forces his entire length in me in one go. The veins in his cock rub against my sensitive folds in a way I've never felt before. I have to admit, his cock is the perfect size. Wide enough to make me feel full, but not too long that he hurts me by pushing all the way into me. I feel ashamed to admit I've dreamed about him taking me in a love making session. He doesn't need to know that, though.

"So wet for me, Little Warrior." I growl at him and his only reply is to laugh at me. My hand comes up to slap him, but he gathers both my hands in one of his, forcing them over my head. This makes my boobs pop upward as my back arches to accommodate the position he now holds me in.

"Only b..." He kisses me, cutting my words off. That silken tongue of his delves into my mouth, claiming me. Refusing to let me breathe for more than a second, he kisses me until I lose my own train of thought.

The longer I'm here with him, well, all three of them, the more I become submissive to them. This makes them think they can get away with this treatment. His mouth moves down my throat and I whimper. He peppers soft kisses all the way to the back of my throat, near my ear. He bites my earlobe as his cock thrusts into me—deep. I moan, unable to stop myself from showing him just how much I'm enjoying this.

"That's my warrior. Let go and allow it to happen." His

tempo quickens, pulsing inside of me and before I can control it, I cum. I don't mean to. It comes out of left field as he bites down on my collarbone, drawing blood. He howls and spills deep within me. I tremble as he sucks my blood and finishes himself off inside me.

"Come sweet one, let's get cleaned up." I wonder why he's acting nice. I shudder as we make it to the bathroom. Hypnos sits me down on the toilet and I look up at him. He takes his wet cock and pushes it toward my mouth.

"Pee, Charlotte. You know you need to." I blush at his crass words. I shake my head, but he holds my head, forcing himself down my throat. I gag, forgetting I'm on the toilet. Instead, I push against his thighs, hoping to dislodge him to no avail. He spills his cum into my mouth while I struggle.

"Fuck, you're taking my piss, such a damn turn on. I'm ready to fuck you again. Drink it all." His words register, causing me to stop struggling in extreme shock. He...he's peeing in my mouth. *Disgusting.* He holds me down on his cock to the point that my throat starts burning. I try with all my might to pull back. The more I struggle, the harder he forces me to accept every drop of his urine.

Hot tears stream down my face as the lights go out. I flinch as he lets out a string of curse words. Pushing my head backward, he takes his cock out of my mouth. This gives me all the time I need. Without a second thought, I push him with all my might. His grip on my hair loosens and he trips, probably over those unzipped pants of his. I can't see so I'm not too sure.

I hear the impact of his head against the wall, a sickening thwack that makes my stomach lurch. The lights flash and suddenly everything seems like it's in slow motion. His eyes go wide as he hits the wall, closing as he falls and crumples to the ground. My brain takes a moment to grasp the concept he—he's old cold. I toe his chest. "Hy... Hypnos?"

When he doesn't move, I jump into action. I run to the closet and grab a shirt and pants. I find two shoes, both canvas material—I don't care if they match or not and it doesn't matter that the sizing is definitely off. I bolt from the room. The lights flash again, this time staying off. The sound of rushing water should make me pause, but then I see it. Water bursting from the walls. I don't understand. I don't care. I run down the stairs and hope like hell I can find the front door.

Freedom is right there. Right freaking there. I sprint full speed into the hallway and turn left. I go to the first door that looks like it *could* be the front door and I yank it open. Trees everywhere. The forest scares me but not as much as these three men scare me. It's an irrational fear and I know this. "Come on Charlotte. Let's get the hell out of here." I give myself a pep talk and run out into the night.

To Be Continued...

ACKNOWLEDGMENTS

Thank you Tori Ellis for sticking with me and keeping my book in line with editing. Also, thank you for being honest and kind. You are amazing.

Thank you Cady Verdiramo for not only coming through for my book cover, but for making me cry with joy and awe at what great work you have done.

Thank you Justine Piquery for being my personal assistant and helping me grow. Your friendship and keeping me sane through all this, means a lot.

Thank you to my cousin B, this book would be nothing without your input and enthusiasm to see more.

ABOUT THE AUTHOR

Hey everyone, thank you for downloading Psychos In Love Book One. Book Two is on preorder now. Link coming soon!

Want to get the latest and most up to date information? Head over to https://www.ransomsbookreviews.com

Let's connect:
Facebook: www.facebook.com/authorsjransom
Instagram: www.instagram.com/authorsjransom
TikTok: www.tiktok.com/authorsjransom

CPSIA information can be obtained
at www.ICGtesting.com
Printed in the USA
BVHW050204090223
658191BV00031B/1014

9 781088 054765